Fare
Game

Tracey Ann Clements

FOR HAROLD

UPCOMING IN 2017/18

By the Book

Irish Times

Norwegian Blue

A Jim Swimmer Christmas

CONTENTS

1
HOMECOMING

Jim Swimmer stared into a full-length mirror and sighed. He didn't register his own haggard reflection, but focussed on the room behind him; dark wooden furniture, a faded patchwork quilt pulled tautly across an antique bedstead, ornate glass bottles arranged on a Victorian-style dressing table. The room was his parent's bedroom and, he supposed, it always would be even though they both passed away during the first quarter of that year. It was now October and although the daylight hours were gradually diminishing the sense of loss was not. Jim knew that he should be grateful as there had been no tragedy, no protracted illness or suffering; they just quietly succumbed to old age within a month of each other, following a life reasonably well lived. Somehow, that didn't make the bereavement easier to bear. Jim looked down at the oriental style rug beneath his feet and felt like an interloper. Maybe it was a combination of tiredness and stress that made him feel this way, he thought, as he had been driving in the dark for several hours. Although the family house was usually no more than a two-hour drive from his home on the outskirts of London, traffic conditions and diversions had extended his journey somewhat and after a long day spent packing up belongings and tying up loose ends he felt mentally and physically drained.

Following the death of his parents, Jim and his elder sister, Sarah, had inherited most of the estate between them. The elderly Swimmers were pragmatic, and on their passing they had expected the house to be sold and the profits to be divided between their two children. 'When we are gone,' they used to say, 'use the money to live your life the way you want; travel the world, take an extended break, be creative; you only have one life, don't spend it thinking 'what if'....' But for some reason this selfless consideration merely made Jim more attached to his parent's life and memory and to the house he grew up in. It was decided, with the assistance of a solicitor friend, that Sarah, recently divorced but settled with her job and children, would have the money from the estate plus a few sentimental items. Jim would inherit 23 Badger Mews, the family house in small town Brockford- with the proviso that things would be evened out should the house be sold with an excessive level of profit. The arrangement was informal, but the siblings generally maintained a good relationship even if they didn't meet up in person very often. It had taken several months to organise personal and practical matters, but now he was here for the foreseeable future with no clear plan. He had arranged to let his London flat fully furnished, so he did have a safety net if it didn't work out. He wondered if the person that would soon be living in his former home would feel as he did now, perhaps they would stand in his bedroom and look at his modern furniture and contemporary lighting and feel like an intruder. Probably not, he decided, because they were strangers and his city residence was devoid of personality and history in the sense that his parent's home was. Well, difficult as it was to envisage, it was his home now, he supposed.

Jim's unease was such that he thought about sleeping in one of the smaller, less cluttered bedrooms, but the effort required to make up a bed for himself after his arduous journey soon condemned that idea. Instead he compromised and lay on top of his parent's heirloom bedspread, fully clothed, and soon fell into a deep sleep.

Jim Swimmer woke earlier than planned the next morning; because of the tiredness that afflicted him the night before it became evident that he had forgotten to close the heavily embossed velvet curtains. Light streamed in through the bay window, exposing dust particles in the air above him. He got up and walked through the house as if he were the new caretaker, the floorboards creaking as he made his way, stopping now and then to look at a picture and smiling to himself. This was an older person's home, he thought, and despite the dust free surfaces and faint smell of furniture polish something about the house felt like a musty museum. Random thoughts and questions went through his mind. 'Why did two people living alone with only sporadic visitors need so many glasses?' 'There are a lot of lamps in this house.' 'Do people still use aerosol spray furniture polish? Do they still sell it in shops?' There were photographs in frames scattered all over the house; ancient-looking black and white wedding photographs, oddly tinged shop developed pictures of Jim and Sarah as children and studio prints taken when they both eventually became university graduates, then more recent school photographs of the two grandchildren, images of his parents over the years, usually with the garden in full summer bloom as the backdrop…While growing up, Jim almost believed that his parents had never been young. John and Sylvie Swimmer were kind and well respected members of the community; intelligent and accommodating, with two well-mannered children. They sounded dull on paper, but then Jim was never a lively type, preferring adult conversations and books from an early age, and so he had a happy and settled childhood. He was now approaching his mid-forties, which was the age his parents were when he was born. They seemed much older than most of his friend's parents, but it never bothered him, unless one of his peers noticed and made an unnecessary comment. He sometimes wondered if his nieces thought of him that way. The old uncle, older than other uncles. Maybe not; was it not the norm to have children later in life nowadays? Jim had never entertained the possibility that he might one day be a father himself; as a younger man, he felt, he was too self- centred, and as an older person he had become too insular and was beset with anxiety about his capability to be responsible for anyone other than himself. Regardless, he had never met anyone he could settle down with and he was happy just to take on the role of the 'geeky' uncle who could please his nieces by fixing their internet issues and talking about the latest apps and devices. Sometimes he wondered if they were just humouring him, but he liked to believe that they truly liked him and tolerated his awkwardness around the younger generation as the eccentricity of a childless uncle.

Jim was plagued by indecisiveness. The decision to hand in his notice to his employer and move back to his childhood home was a rare impulsive action, although he had no choice if he wanted to keep the old family house for himself- and he knew that he wasn't ready to let it go just yet. And so, one rainy day towards the end of June, the time had come to make it official and from then onwards there could be no turning back. It had been a strange month; Jim had turned forty-four on the same day that the UK had voted to leave the EU via the referendum. Although, like many Londoners, he voted against Brexit, he took this as a sign that he was doing the right thing; as the UK decided to exit so would he, no matter what the consequences might be. He couldn't have predicted the ensuing political resignations, which were much more dramatic than his quiet, largely unnoticed exit. He just knew that he didn't want to reach forty-five and still be feeling that he had wasted his life, had achieved nothing, was going nowhere. The few people that he confided in told him that he was insane to give up a well-paid job in central London; they warned him that he was making a huge mistake and would be sabotaging his career. Although well intentioned, this lack of support made him feel more isolated and determined to move on. Jim waited nervously outside the office with the clear glass door, just for a few seconds as he didn't want to be seen lingering. He had booked a slot in the online calendar, but regardless he popped his head around the door and politely enquired whether his boss,

Alistair Thornton, had a minute or two to spare.

He was silently waved in and sat down, clutching the envelope containing his resignation letter and desperately trying to recall the speech he had rehearsed over and over in his head the night before.

'So,' Thornton asked in his monotonous, rather loud voice. 'How is Jim Swimmer getting along?

'Drowning,' he thought, 'sinking lower and lower the longer I stay here…' But he forced a smile and calmly replied.

'Can't complain. Enjoying the better weather and the lighter evenings.'

He cringed as he remembered that it had been raining relentlessly all day, but instead of correcting himself he continued with his prepared speech, explaining that he had to return to his home town to deal with family matters which could take some time.

It was strange, he thought, that like so many others he often thought about the prospect of resigning, of leaving the office triumphantly knowing the there was an imminent end to the daily routine, where time and skill is measured in purely monetary terms. This fantasy did not include his lengthy notice period and the seemingly endless list of tasks to pass on to his replacement. Thornton was uncharacteristically sympathetic and accommodating, offering a sabbatical or a period of extended leave. Jim suddenly felt guilty, but held his ground as a complete break was what he needed, and thirty minutes later his resignation had been accepted and his leaving date and handover plan was agreed in principle. Then it was back to work and no one was any the wiser, just another Monday morning with deadlines to meet and a constant stream of emails demanding a response. The next three months seemed to progress slowly, until the final week of his employment when he suddenly had so many loose ends to tie up and introductions to make that he feared he would not be able to leave as scheduled. However, once he accepted that this would be his successor's concern, and that he had done all he could, he started to look forward to making the break. At the end of his last day Jim went for a quiet farewell drink with a few of his colleagues before excusing himself as he had a lot to sort out. It was not long before he completely forgot all about his old work environment. Although he felt slightly guilty about not working for the time being, the sense of freedom was temporarily invigorating and, he thought, taking time out to re-evaluate his life would have been something that his parents would have approved of.

Jim's respect for his parents was his driving force in life; no matter what he did they had been proud, small achievements were acknowledged, the ordinariness of his life was something they were content with. They were never heard to be judgemental, common decency and respect trumped money and status every time… a far cry from the competitive, target driven society prevalent in London. Apart from school teachers and most doctors, they were the only ones to call him James and he rather liked that. Jim's father was a traditional academic type and tended to refer to people by their surnames so this intimate yet still slightly formal method of address somehow pleased him. Maybe that was why he felt he needed to come home; the last time he could remember being truly happy and content with life was when he was at home, with his family and friends, in Brockford.

However, at this moment he felt that he needed to freshen up and escape from the claustrophobic confines of the house, which felt a little too warm despite the chilly October weather outside. The central heating timer had been programmed to ensure that all the radiators came on during the early hours of the morning; Jim would need to reset the schedule to suit his own preferences later. After a brief struggle to operate the shower correctly, Jim was soon properly awake and dressed, ready to face his first day in Brockford. He decided that he needed to go out and reacquaint himself with the area, and see what had changed over the years. Although he had been back to his home town many times in recent years, the primary focus of these fleeting visits was always to spend time with his parents, and as they were so much older they didn't like to go out too much. They preferred to spend time in the garden, sitting on the patio with a cup of tea and a slice of lemon drizzle cake while pointing out the rhododendrons or other plant life. Sometimes they could be persuaded to go for a brief walk in the woods that backed onto their property, where they enjoyed noting the changing seasons and looking out for signs of wildlife. In short, they liked home comforts and the simple things in life.

Jim soon found himself standing in the old-fashioned kitchen, which was a decent size by modern standards. It wasn't the biggest room in the house but it was the most well used and was always warm and cosy despite the old tiled floor. It was dominated by a large oak table, where various people had sat and discussed the state of the world, ruminated over their personal and family problems and shared happy memories and dubious anecdotes. The quietness now was eerie, but Jim still had the thought in his mind that his mother had really been on holiday and would walk in at any moment, wearing her checked winter coat and carrying several bags full of shopping. He could envision her restocking the fridge and cupboards, talking about who and what she had seen without looking over her shoulder to see if anyone were listening, as was her way. He didn't realise that his parents had switched to online shopping as a necessity in their later years, when driving was no longer a safe or practical option, although he was pleased that his octogenarian parents were forward thinking enough to get to grips with the internet. He was unaware of the extra duties that Rosie, their carer and domestic help, had undertaken to keep his parents presentable, thinking of her more as a family friend who popped in now and again to help with essential tasks and to keep them company. His parents were proud, and his visits brief, so his memory of them as independent and responsible individuals was preserved.

Jim stood in the centre of the room, looked around nervously, and wondered for a moment what he had let himself in for. The house was large and homely, but a far cry from his London flat, where he had everything set up as he needed it. Everything in his own place was 'smart'; the heating, lighting, shower, plug sockets…all controlled by mobile apps or his favourite voice activated technology. He had started researching smart security too, but there was little point in a property with a twenty-four-hour concierge. Here, although he had reasonable internet access, everything was comparatively primitive, with very few gadgets or gizmos. He smiled as he remembered how excited his mother had once been to have acquired an electric tin opener. That must have been the late seventies. Or was it the eighties? Of course, she had used it a few times and then it was forgotten about; too much trouble to bother with. No, although retro was fun now and then Jim would never want to go back to the days of fixing cassette tapes with a pen and some sticky tape. Not when he could say a few words and the music of his choice would instantly play. He would consider upgrading to a faster internet connection and set up his voice activated Reverb Smart Home device as soon as possible, he decided.

Jim hadn't had a chance to go shopping yet, so he settled for a cup of black coffee before going out to the driveway and removing suitcases and boxes from his car. He cautiously moved the heavy iron doorstop to prevent the old front door from slamming shut and locking him out, just as his parents had in the past. He had arrived late the previous night and only had the energy to unpack the essentials. He could have been going on holiday, for he mostly just brought clothes, toiletries and a few personal effects. Almost everything that Jim owned was downloaded, or 'in the cloud': he owned no DVDs, games or compact discs, everything was paperless, most his books were in digital format. The few possessions that he had not loaded into his car were placed into storage for the time being. Once he had deposited his belongings to his satisfaction he checked the cupboards in order to ascertain what he might need to buy. In the fridge, he found fresh milk and butter, and cursed himself for not checking before. He realised that it must have been left by Rosie, who was still employed to maintain the house while it was empty and would have been aware of his imminent arrival. A nice gesture, he thought, although the idea of another person with a key who could come in at any time did unnerve him a little. Maybe it was something he would have to reassess later. 'All lights off!' he said habitually as he flicked the light switch to the off position. No matter how much he talked to the house, it never responded…but old habits die hard and he continued to speak to it nonetheless.

Jim closed the old wooden front door behind him, and his mind flashed back to when he was young and would be the first to leave the house in the morning, usually to make his way to school or college. He now wished he had worn a warmer jacket, as Brockford seemed to be several degrees colder than he was used to. As a rule, he always checked the weather forecast with 'Holly', the name or 'wake word' he had assigned to his Reverb Smart Home Hub, before venturing into the outside world. He laughed out loud at the absurdity of his dependency on technology, then quickly looked around to ensure that no loitering neighbours had overheard. Luckily, the street was deserted, although Jim was sure that the curtains were twitching in the house opposite. It was a rarity, he thought, as he jiggled the key in the Yale lock, to still have such an old-fashioned door. It was painted a dark green colour, with the '23' in gold-plated numbers screwed securely above the well-polished but slightly green brass knocker. Should he change it for something more practical, without draughty gaps and the need for so much upkeep? He would think about that later. He could maybe see what Sarah thought when she came down to go through his parents remaining belongings with him. They had wanted to set aside an entire weekend, knowing that there was a lot to sort out and that they would constantly be distracted by memories, photographs, and most likely a random stream of visitors once word was out that Sarah was visiting. However, she could only spare a day so they would have to do as much as possible in the time they had. Sarah was so much more of a people person, he thought, she had a naturally friendly face and was easy to talk to. He was envious of her confidence and cheerful disposition, and of how people viewed her, but at the end of the day you are who you are and pretending to be any different is just a falsehood that will always be exposed in the end. He would always be quiet, serious Jim no matter how much he tried to change, but he was always eager to please and he knew that he placed more importance on being liked than he should. But this was a new start for him, and he was determined to be easy going and to try to have a more positive attitude.

Once the door was securely locked he walked to his car, which was parked at a slightly odd angle in the gravel driveway. He drove a dark grey Prius, which made sense in London where hybrid vehicles were exempt from the congestion charge but which seemed to invoke curiosity and negative comments elsewhere. No matter how many times he explained that it was a hybrid, and that the battery was charged by the braking action, he would always be asked where he plugged it in, followed by cheeky comments about getting a 'real car.' Jim liked the quietness of the engine and, after all, a car was just a means of getting from A to B…he had no time for all the jargon associated with motoring and would choose not to drive if this were a viable option. At this precise moment, he was glad of the car's heating system, and he sat there in silence for a few minutes, deciding what music to play, opted for the second movement of Beethoven's Symphony No 7- one of his father's favourites- and then drove away prudently, quietly confident that he would be able to locate the supermarket carpark in the centre of the town.

He drove through the streets of Brockford, noticing a lot that was familiar, but also some major changes. He suddenly realised that he was driving down the street where Nova Anderssen used to live, and abruptly slowed his speed to a delicate crawl. Nova was his soul mate when he was a teenager; never actually his girlfriend but, apart from in the physical sense, they could not have been closer. They knew each other inside out, shared their deepest thoughts and fears and were inseparable for those formative years. It seemed inconceivable, but they had drifted apart over time. After college, Nova wanted to attend some sort of librarianship course, and the best option at that time was a university in the north of England. He had studied English Literature at a new university at the other end of the country, and had missed her dreadfully but was never able to articulate that feeling. He had envisaged her meeting new and exciting people; she was bright and attractive, and would easily make friends. He didn't want to get in the way, be an obstruction as she made her way in the world. In contrast, he had made a few good friends while studying, but had lost touch with them all within ten years, only later reconnecting online and never in person. Jim often wished that he had applied to the same university and moved away with her; if she had asked him he would have followed her without hesitation. But the suggestion was never made and he was too uncertain to make the first move.

As Jim continued past her former home, he thought that he could see someone moving about inside the house, but he was unable to stop and look properly as a large white car was waiting impatiently behind him, the engine revving aggressively, so he had no option but to move on swiftly. To his knowledge, Nova's father, Professor Anderssen, still lived there and he had last spoken to him at his father's funeral six months ago. Jim felt that he should call in, for old times' sake, but he had heard that the Professor was seriously ill and it wouldn't be right to turn up uninvited under these circumstances. After all, the Professor had been a widower for many years and had become accustomed to his own routines, he told himself, looking for more reasons to justify this decision. It is strange, thought Jim, that he always referred to him as the Professor, or Professor Anderssen, never by his first name of Lars, after all these years. Nova always called his own parents John and Sylvie, like everyone else they knew. The Professor had been a very influential man of science in his day, travelling from his native Oslo with his wife Anna and their two children to take up a variety of positions at Universities all over Europe and, prior to the move to England, America. In a town like Brockford, the Nordic settlers were considered exotic- maybe it would be the same anywhere in England during the early eighties? Thinking about it, the Professor's eclectic dress sense may have influenced how people regarded him. Nova herself was tall, slim and naturally blonde, with fair skin that always reminded Jim of the porcelain tea set that his mother kept for special occasions, or maybe one of those scary china dolls that his sister used to collect; anyway, she looked very different when compared to the local girls. This, he often thought, was why they became friends; neither of them fitted in. She was self-confident but stood out physically and culturally, while Jim was serious and shy, mature and quietly intelligent, tall but somehow unnoticeable, almost invisible. Together they always seemed to create a sense of balance. In addition, Jim's parents were also academic types, albeit on a totally different level. Dr John Swimmer was a historian and he had been published in his younger days, but by his mid-forties he had lost interest in writing and research and was content just to plod along as a lecturer until he reached retirement age. He never used the title of 'Doctor' outside of his workplace; sometimes he said that this was because he feared he would be mistaken for a medical doctor but other times he just said it was not important to him. Jim and Sarah agreed that it was likely down to modesty. Sylvie Swimmer was intelligent and had attended university but didn't go out to work once she became a mother, although she was well-read and often involved in local political and social matters.

Professor Anderssen, like John Swimmer, took a position in the University located approximately thirty minutes away; Brockford was commutable and property was reasonably priced. Therefore, it was a convenient location for staff to live but, aside from the woodland and coastal areas, students had no real reason to visit. There were now a fair amount of shops; mostly the same ones as you would find in all the cloned high streets in England alongside a handful of independent stores. Jim parked sensibly in a bay in the corner of the busy carpark, made a mental note of the time, and decided to see if he could find some warmer, casual clothes to buy; maybe even a new coat. He intended to go for a walk every day, if the weather wasn't too unfriendly and he needed to eradicate any excuses that he might come up with. This took longer than expected, as his indecisiveness had unexpectedly returned with a vengeance, but eventually he forced himself to make some random choices and was relieved to discover the Jazz Bean Cafe, which sold half decent coffee and freshly made sandwiches. As he was leaving the café just over an hour later, he felt a hand on his back and turned to face Julian Green, an old schoolfriend who was the same age as his sister and, if he recalled correctly, had also been her boyfriend for a brief time when they were teenagers. Even though Jim had been all over town that day, this was the first person he saw that he knew, and he couldn't deny that it was good to see a friendly face.

'I saw you through the window- can't talk now,' Julian said, 'but I will be in The Highwayman this evening, around six o clock, if you have time to catch up? Maybe grab a bite to eat?'

Jim had no plans at all and welcomed an excuse not to cook, so agreed without hesitation and said, quite truthfully, that he would look forward to it. He walked on, and put his clothing purchases in the boot of the car. The three hours parking allowance was almost up, so he relocated his car into a smaller car park just around the corner. He then took his time browsing in the supermarket for store cupboard essentials and a few items that he would need for the house, before heading back to Badger Mews.

The next-door neighbour was standing by the silver car in her driveway as Jim arrived home. She smiled and waved as she saw him so he felt obliged to wander over and say hello. Jim's detached house was the last building in the cul de sac, so the only people that passed directly by were those on foot requiring access to the woodland area. The pathway to the woods was adjacent to the garden boundary fence, but fortunately it was somewhat overgrown and not lit at night so very few people used it. Chance meetings here were few and far between, so Jim thought that he should try to be sociable. The neighbour clearly didn't have much time to spare but was friendly, introducing herself as Donna and saying that she had only moved in recently. She worked locally, for the council, and her husband, Steve, had a landscaping business. They had two young daughters, who she had to pick up from school about five minutes ago…Jim took the hint and said they would speak another time. As he unpacked the car for the second time that day, he contemplated the garden and the problems he might have. He had been a city dweller for almost all his adult life, and certainly didn't have green fingers. If Steve was as friendly as his wife he might be able to get some advice; maybe he would be able to recommend a local gardener.

Jim spent a couple of hours going through the contents of the house, and was relieved when he noticed that it was almost time to meet Julian Green. He was feeling hungry, so after a quick change of clothes he eagerly made his way to the local pub. As he parked the Prius in the dimly lit car park he thought back to the old days, when drinking laws were pretty much the same but much less enforced by publicans, or police for that matter. No need for a fake ID, no questions were asked. He double locked the car, just to be safe, and resolved to have a relaxing evening as he walked across the tarmac.

2

THE HIGHWAYMAN INN

'Still the same creaky old sign,' Jim thought, as he approached the main entrance to The Highwayman Inn. He was relieved when he stepped inside and saw that Julian Green was already present and had secured a table in a quiet corner, next to an open fire which was crackling quietly and creating a homely feeling at odds with the public nature of the building. Julian sipped his drink and they looked through the menu; standard pub fayre, so they both ordered the Turpin Burger, which came with beer battered onion rings and a drink as standard. Jim initially ordered a coke to go with his meal, explaining to his old friend that he was driving.

'You can have one beer!' stated Julian, 'You can trust me, I'm a copper remember...'

Jim did remember; when Julian joined the force a few of their friends weren't exactly supportive and this was a sore point, so he compromised and opted for a lager shandy and then made a point of asking him how his career was developing, and was careful to maintain an interest in the response. Despite being in his mid-forties, Julian was no longer ambitious, and he was content to stay at the rank of Detective Constable, preferring to spend time with his family rather than chase promotion. He had no intention of leaving Brockford and there were only so many positions available, after all. He lamented the lack of resources available, and explained how they didn't always attend when minor crimes were reported. There simply wasn't the manpower any more, and the administrative work was never ending. Jim remembered reading something along these lines a while back; did an official tell people to investigate crimes themselves, or something similar? Ask for neighbour's CCTV footage, trawl pawnshops in search of stolen belongings, things like that... Inevitably, the conversation came around to Jim, and what he was doing now that he was back; how long would he be staying, what was his plan? He didn't want to say that he didn't have a firm plan so had to improvise and said that he was writing a book.

'Hah, I knew it!' exclaimed Julian. 'You always were gifted in that department…Remember when you won that essay award at school? So, what's the book about?'

Jim again had to think on his feet, and came up with the first genre that came into his head.

'Detective fiction. It's about a police detective in a town very much like Brockford…Erm, his name is…Maitland...' decided Jim, looking around the bar for inspiration and chancing on a name from a poster.

Well, it was now.

Jim elaborated: 'Maitland is a serious type, career minded and a bit of a loner, but has a sixth sense when it comes to the criminal mind. He operates as the main law enforcer in a small town but, although his name will be plastered across the front cover, he's more there to facilitate the narrative than to be a fully developed character really, he is cold and detached, like a cardboard cut-out, and merely allows us access to things we normally wouldn't see… its more Brockford Noir than Midsomer Murders, it is the perpetrators or victim's viewpoint that interests me, and it is this that I want to engage with, to examine the grey areas …'

Jim thought it would appear obvious that he was rambling inanely and making things up on the spot, but Julian seemed genuinely interested. In fact, he became quite animated, which may have had something to do with the beer he had drunk, and brazenly suggested that Jim could name the detective after him; in return he could give him some ideas for plotlines and so on.

'Ok,' said Jim. 'I will even give you a promotion- I'll call him Sergeant Maitland Green, but I should change quite a few things, don't want him to resemble you too much, you know, don't want to get sued by your wife or the police force! And, anyway, Maitland is so detached, he is almost a sociopath; you are nothing like him in that sense.'

Jim told Julian that he wanted to incorporate technology into Maitland Green's crime solving methodology; he would be a contemporary de*tech*tive of sorts. Jim had also read somewhere that people could record crimes in progress and send it straight to the police via a standard 999 call, but this was not something that he knew much about. Brockford residents, after all, were still debating the merits of CCTV and speed cameras and, in some cases, neighbourhood watch was considered a step too far. It wasn't long before their food arrived, and there was a brief lull in the conversation as the two men enjoyed their meals. The Turpin Burger was substantial, and Julian laughed as Jim tried to ascertain the most efficient way to eat it, telling him that he had been out of town for far too long. Still, Jim managed to clear his plate although he felt that he might not need to eat again for a week.

They talked for a few more hours, about the old days and what had changed, about families and small town life. Julian ribbed Jim for looking almost the same as he did over twenty years ago and he swore that he was still wearing the same clothes as well, while Jim poked fun at Julian's newly acquired beard and suggested that he was morphing into a slightly more modern version of his father, which wasn't denied. Julian didn't mention Nova; this surprised Jim as they were all part of the same group of friends and she was very close to her father so it was a given that she would have been back in town on multiple occasions. Although he was more than interested to find out if Julian had any information, Jim couldn't quite bring himself to broach the subject.

At nine thirty, they both decided that it was time to call it a night. As they stood up Jim noted that Julian was a couple of inches taller than him, which made him feel less self-conscious regarding his own stature. Although they had known each other for a long time, they had never been close friends, probably due to the small age difference which was significant when they were teenagers but was no longer noticeable. Jim was pleasantly surprised by how well they now got along. He supposed that they were different people now. Two almost middle aged men: one married with two lively children and a responsible job, the other single, unattached with an abandoned career and responsible only for himself. But each admired and was envious of the other to some extent.

'Do you know,' remarked Julian as they walked towards the door that led to The Highwayman Inn's almost deserted carpark. 'The new recruits at the station don't know what a highwayman is, or was, or whatever. Never even heard of Dick Turpin, or Adam Ant for that matter. They all think that a highwayman is just someone who fixes the roads.'

Jim smiled, and paused, gesturing towards the front of the building before responding.

'I thought the picture on the sign might give it away?'

Julian had left his car at home, so Jim offered him a lift. It was only a few minutes along the road, and as he got out of the car directly opposite his house Julian took out his mobile phone and asked for Jim's phone number, which he deftly saved while suggesting they meet up for a few drinks once he had settled in properly.

'Don't forget, I can give you some ideas for Maitland Green, or if you need any advice regarding procedures and stuff, I'm your man. Oh, and one more thing- a Prius- seriously? When are you going to grow up and get a real car!'

At this point, Jim acknowledged to himself that he would probably end up writing that book, if only to satisfy his friend and to prove that he could complete a project, and regretted not saying he was writing a science fiction novel. That would have been much easier. *Brockford 2060. A future where all human interaction is through digital media and people lose the ability to communicate face to face. A dystopian novel in the vein of 'We' or 'Brave New World' or '1984', but in this future, there is no dictator, no one is in control but by the time someone realises this it is too late; society heads blindly into destruction...* Clichéd and contrived; no one would be interested in following up on that, but it was too late now. Wasn't that something E M Forster wrote about in the early part of the twentieth century? He would have to look that up when he remembered. As he pulled away, he couldn't resist the temptation to play 'Stand and Deliver' through his Bluetooth car speakers, very loudly. There was nothing wrong with his car, or the integrated sound system. He had been a young boy when the song first came out in the early eighties, surely it wasn't as bad as he remembered...he concluded that it was, but listened to the end of the song anyway.

3
NOCTURNAL GUEST

Jim arrived home around ten o clock and went into the kitchen to make some tea. Whilst the kettle was slowly coming to the boil on the stove he opened the cupboard by the window to take out his large mug with the hand-painted snow scene; it was a Christmas gift from an aunt living abroad when he was twelve years old, and he had been using it ever since. His parents had always kept it there for him when he visited, and he didn't have the heart to tell them that he preferred to drink from a plain white mug. It was starting to show its age now, with hairline cracks and faded paint. 'A bit like me', he thought to himself and half smiled. He noticed a light in the summer house at the end of the garden and knew instantly who was there. He continued to make the tea and decided he ought to greet his nocturnal visitor, hesitating to consider the etiquette of such an action. Should he take a drink to his visitor? He formed an image in his mind of himself struggling along the garden path in the dark with a fully loaded tray- for who knew how his guest would take his tea, or if he even liked tea- but decided this was not a viable option. Instead he picked up his cup with one hand and with the other grabbed the torch left by the back door and made his way cautiously along the overgrown pathway, stepping carefully to avoid, as far as possible, the slugs and snails congregating beside the damp grass, which had grown unkempt and erratic within a relatively short space of time. Jim had no interest in gardening, so he would need to hire someone to help if he was still here come Spring- which was seeming very likely.

Walter, an elderly, well-dressed man who looked to be in his early eighties, was sitting in front of a chess set, carefully and deliberately manoeuvring the pieces into a starting position. He looked up as Jim entered, and smiled warmly. Jim's father had, for as long as he could remember, made his way down to the summerhouse to meet his friend and played chess late into the night. It was just one of those things that had always happened, without explanation or ever being questioned. John Swimmer had suffered frequent bouts of insomnia, and Jim had inherited that tendency, often sitting up late into the night, reading or watching old films, sometimes going for a drive if he were particularly restless. Now, it seemed, Walter was waiting for him.

'I always knew you would come back at some point, James. I hope you don't mind me being here, it is a little unusual I know. Most irregular. But you must say if you have something that you need to be doing- no one wants to be a nuisance.'

Jim replied that he was welcome at any time, as one of his father's oldest friends, but went on to explain that he was a poor fit for John Swimmer's shoes, if that was what he was thinking, as he was certainly not a competent chess player; he could barely remember the basic rules.

Walter laughed, quietly, and explained that neither he nor his father were anywhere near grandmaster level, pausing momentarily before continuing to elaborate.

'Your father,' he said, 'was technically very proficient, but lacked the killer instinct required to successfully complete the end game. I myself have little skill but have an unmatched determination to keep going when it seems all is lost. It's a family trait. Your father is like Carl Schlechter, the World Champion that never was, known for his drawn games, a gentleman in every respect. A game between the two of us could go on for weeks, even though he was clearly the superior player. Your father and I, of course, not Herr Schlechter and myself- I am neither that old nor that well connected. You, he told me, are a capable player but have a tendency to over think and too often will second guess your strategy- usually unnecessarily. In chess and in life, you should always trust your instincts and go with your initial impulse. Don't be too afraid to make a mistake; it is how we learn.'

Jim thought that he had a valid point, but said nothing. He was actively trying to be more impulsive but it was not easy. Then again, he was sitting in a summer house late at night, preparing to play chess for the first time in years- with a man that he barely knew, with whom he had only ever exchanged a few polite words in passing. Jim could have made an excuse, said he was tired or had work to do, was expecting a phone call, but he didn't. Again, he realised that he was analysing a choice after it was already made and immediately resolved to look outside himself and focus on the man in front of him.

Jim noted how Walter always used more words than were necessary, and he appreciated this as it reminded him of his father, who had a similar habit. Jim sat in his father's chair, and chose the black pawn ensconced within

Walter's wrinkled hand, and they started a game which should only have taken a few minutes but which took almost half an hour with the constant pauses as the two men talked about old times and about Jim's current situation.

As expected, Walter won the first game easily, and then immediately returned the pieces to their starting positions and began again, without seeking Jim's consent for a second game or deviating from the course of the conversation. Walter, it seemed, knew everything about everyone in Brockford, past and present. If he were a woman, Jim thought, he would be called a gossip, but nevertheless Walter was a natural storyteller and time passed quickly. Jim played better on the second game, although he later wondered if this was because his old, rather limited skills were coming back to him or, as seemed more likely, Walter was being deliberately careless and providing his weak opponent with multiple opportunities to gain an advantage. That was something his father would never have done; John Swimmer was not one to spare a person's feelings. Not that he was callous or hard-hearted, but he considered it his job to prepare his children for the real world. Whenever Jim or Sarah would declare 'It's not fair!', as children of their generation inevitably would on many occasions, he would rarely intervene and typically reply with the standard response of 'life's not fair.' Following his third consecutive defeat, Jim realised that more than two hours had passed and so said goodnight before heading back to the house, realising that he now knew a lot more about Brockford and its residents but, strangely, nothing more about Walter.

4
CHANCE MEETING

Initially Jim Swimmer envisioned spending his free time leisurely, but soon grew bored and craved a new challenge. He had always worked long hours and tended to obsess over every little detail of a project until it was completed. He sat in front of his laptop and thought about making some progress with the detective novel that he had talked about in The Highwayman Inn. After all, he had dreamed of writing a novel since his childhood and had studied literature to Masters level. Maybe the time wasn't right to create his masterpiece, but metaphorically putting pen to paper would be a start. Julian had sent, via email, the details of a competition for first time authors who had never been published, and he read carefully through the advice from the judges regarding what they were looking for. The main stumbling block, he felt, was the need for likeable characters, or at least a protagonist that readers could empathise with. He started out fine, but every happy go lucky character he created eventually fell into a pattern of, if not misery, extreme negativity. He felt himself being consumed by this same attitude, as if he was being pulled into a vacuum, and he didn't want to be that person. This was a fresh start; a chance to change his outlook and find a lifestyle that would suit his personality. A way forward, so to speak. So, he decided that he take a break from writing for the time being, but he would continue to work on characters and plots. He needed to get out and about and meet people with the intention of developing some new ideas. Maybe, he thought, he would be ready in a couple of weeks to make a start on the Maitland Green stories; he just needed some more inspiration. And so, it turned out that a chance meeting in a local café gave him just the opportunity that he was looking for

Jim had made an agreement with Rosie that she would be employed to do some cleaning and general housework at regular set times, and he always tried to ensure that he was not at home during these sessions. She was trustworthy, he quickly ascertained, and although she was pleasant enough company, except for a fondness for his parents they had little in common. Therefore, as was typical on a Wednesday morning, Jim was sitting at his preferred table in the corner of the Jazz Bean coffee shop in the centre of town, reading an article in one of the complimentary newspapers like a true gentleman of leisure. Although the café had what Julian referred to as 'a hipster vibe' and tended to attract the younger crowds, the coffee was so good that Jim made it his regular haunt. He sensed someone trying to get his attention, and looked up to see who it was. He was sure that he should recognise the portly, slightly balding man smiling and waving at him; he had something familiar about him, but somehow Jim just couldn't place him. The forehead was too large, the eyebrows very unkempt, a stubbly unshaven face…but the dark, deep set eyes and full lips, something about his face was identifiable but slightly amiss. Fortunately, just as the apparent stranger patted him on the shoulder and sat down on the chair opposite, breathing heavily as he did so, Jim had a sudden realisation and could identify Thomas McDougall, the elder brother of an old school- friend, Michael, whom he had not seen for several years. Everyone who lived locally knew the McDougall brothers. Michael, he discovered through Thomas, had moved away for his work more than ten years ago, and was rarely seen in Brockford. Thomas, along with his twin brother Jason, had started up a local taxi company not long after finishing college. Quite an achievement, Jim had said at the time, for the brothers hadn't had many advantages growing up. Seeing how much Thomas had aged since the last time he had seen him made Jim wonder how people from his past saw him nowadays- did they have to look twice and put the clues together before ascertaining who he was? Were they calculating how old he must be now and comparing the reality to their expectations? He wasn't sure why this would matter anyway. Thomas had been quite enamoured with Nova Anderssen as a young man, and chose the name 'Odin's Cars' for the business as he thought this would impress her, maybe appeal to her Nordic roots. A reference, he told her, to the Norse God, who rode his grey eight-legged steed across the sky. At that time, however, Thomas was limited to a silver Ford Escort which, although he drove it much faster than was legally acceptable, would never have got anyone to the underworld- and, it soon transpired, he had even less chance of making an impression on Nova. A few years after starting the business Jason left town suddenly, and no one seemed to know where he had gone or why he had left. Following Jason's abrupt departure, the taxi service was still running with moderate success under the remaining brother's sole management, largely due to the lack of serious competition. Locally, everyone always referred to Toms Taxis, although the sign above the door still read Odin's Cars. Newcomers to Brockford were often initially confused about the company's dual naming, assuming that there were two separate businesses.

As was only polite, Jim enquired after Michael, and was told that he had moved up north where he had a job lined up, married a local girl and had a son, who he had christened Dougall as he couldn't name him after just one of his brothers. Jim raised an eyebrow.

'Dougall McDougall? That's nice…Have you heard from Jason at all?'

Thomas shook his head and rapidly changed the subject, clearly not wishing to discuss the topic.

'What are you up to now?', he asked. 'I heard that you drive a Prius. Good cars, they are, very economical. We are always looking for occasional drivers with their own vehicles if you're ever at a loose end.'

Uber hadn't arrived in town yet so Thomas pretty much had a monopoly. After driving in London, Jim could easily navigate his way around a small town like Brockford, and he was looking for something 'normal' to do; for a reason to leave the house that didn't involve drinking such vast amounts of coffee or imposing on old friends with busy lives. While it was good to catch up with everyone he soon found that most people had routines that they were quite attached to, and he was never one to outstay his welcome.

In London, it was quite common to drive a Prius. Jim was rather fond of his car, which he had owned for a good few years but looked after well. However, in his hometown, especially among his old school-friends, it was an object of friendly derision. He didn't mind too much, as the focus on his choice of car detracted from himself and the fact that he had left a well-paid job in the capital city to move back to a small town with limited opportunities. He wanted a stress-free existence, he would tell people, truthfully; he wanted to be around 'real' people that he could trust, he was fed up with the back stabbing, career obsessed phoneys who could never have an honest conversation. There was always an ulterior motive, a reason behind the reason for every form of contact. He didn't see it as throwing away an education, and to be honest his degree subject had barely any relevance in the area he eventually settled for. There was more to life than money, he argued. He appreciated that he could say that now that financial remuneration wasn't a driving force in any decisions that he made. It was true that he now had the time and patience to read, visit museums and so on. However, he could sense that isolation and solitary activities were not the best thing for someone in his state of mind and not conducive to the creation of the happy go lucky, positive incarnation of Jim Swimmer that he was trying so hard to cultivate. Surely, he thought, talking to customers going from A-B, all with a story to tell, their own narratives, would provide a good foundation for his writing project. He immediately took Thomas up on his offer, which surprised them both. It would take a few weeks to arrange the formalities before he could start work, Thomas explained. This timescale would enable Jim to further familiarise himself with the wider local area, and, although fundamentally unchanged, he had already noted new housing estates and shops that seemed to have appeared overnight and extended the town to a certain degree.

It was Thomas McDougall who told Jim that Nova Anderssen was back in town. Thomas started talking about how busy the bookshop on the High Street was and how he was just about to pick up a coffee for Nova- the Jazz Bean Signature Caramel Cappuccino was her favourite- and take it over on his way back to the taxi office. Jim was suddenly attentive, but had to ask him to repeat what he said. Thomas expressed surprise that Jim was unaware of Nova's presence- after all, he noted drily, they were always so close. Thomas became animated and appeared to enjoy updating Jim regarding the current situation, explaining that the Professor's condition was more serious than at first thought, he was terminally ill, and that Nova had taken some sort of extended leave or left her job, he wasn't sure which, and had moved back to take care of her father. She was helping in the bookshop in the meantime, and looked well considering the circumstances. She was single, as far as Thomas knew- Jim hadn't asked for this information- and she didn't know what her long-term plans were. There was an awkward pause while Thomas waited for a response, but he then promptly decided that he ought to secure a place in the expanding queue and told Jim that he would sort out some paperwork and be in touch if he could just take some contact details. Once information had been exchanged and Thomas had walked away, limping slightly on his left leg, Jim felt an immense sense of relief and found he could breathe easily again. He sat for several minutes and looked down at his rapidly cooling coffee and wondered what had just happened. Nova was back in town, but she hadn't contacted him; did she know he was here? And did he just agree to driving strangers around in his own car?

5
RECONNECTING

It was a couple of weeks before Jim felt he could act on the information that Nova was back in town. He felt embarrassed that he had found out through Thomas McDougall that she was working in a local bookshop and staying with her father in their family home. It was difficult for him to get back in touch because so many years had passed since they had last spoken to each other, although there had been no falling out or bad feeling between them. Every time the landline rung he momentarily thought it would be her, that word had got out that he was home and she wanted to catch up with him. However, she was never on the line, and there were no messages on the answerphone, no missed calls from a local number or a mobile phone. Surely Thomas had mentioned their meeting in the coffee shop? Maybe he had offended her in some way; he should at least have enquired about the Professor when he first arrived. What sort of friend was he? He knew he would have to remedy the situation somehow.

Even after Jim had made the decision to make the first move he didn't feel able to be completely upfront, and planned an elaborate ruse to engineer a 'chance' meeting. He went online and looked up new book releases, found a couple which received favourable reviews and decided to pop in and see if they were in stock, maybe feigning surprise that Nova was working there on that day. And so, one Tuesday, after changing his clothes several times as he wanted to portray the image of someone who is casually going about his day but looks presentable nonetheless, he spent most of the morning in the coffee shop. When he finally found the courage to make the move to the bookshop he found the door locked and a sign on the window which read 'Back in Ten Minutes.' He felt deflated and thought that maybe it was a sign that he should stay away a little bit longer; today was not the day to reconnect. He looked at the window displays and realised that it was Halloween; on one side of the door the focus was on ghost stories and Edgar Allan Poe, and on the other were supernatural characters associated with children's books. Not the right day- he was sure of that, at least. But before he could walk away he heard Nova's voice behind him, first offering an apology for the closure and then expressing surprise at discovering one of her oldest friends standing in front of her. Within a few minutes, they were inside the shop with Nova making coffee and hunting for some elusive biscuits and Jim pretending that he hadn't had a cup of coffee all day while trying to sound convincing about a book that was recommended to him by an acquaintance.

'Did no one tell you I was here?' asked Nova, disregarding his attempts at small talk.

Thomas had clearly not mentioned anything about their meeting in the coffee shop, which seemed a bit strange. One thing Jim could never do convincingly was lie, so he confessed all, and told her that he wanted to see her but it had been so long, and he thought that there might have been a reason that she had not made contact, and she laughed and said that he always did overthink everything- she had been extremely busy and didn't have his contact number, plus she wasn't sure if he was staying at the house alone or with his other half, who might be unhappy about a strange woman turning up on the doorstep…Jim quickly interjected and established his unattached status, then immediately regretted his abrupt interruption, not wishing to sound too eager. Fortunately, Nova smiled coyly and confirmed her position to be the same. In no time at all the initial awkwardness between them had dissipated and they were talking with a frankness and familiarity that made it seem like they had never been apart.

*

Nova Anderssen clearly remembered moving to Brockford when she was 12 years old, along with her school teacher mother Anna, her father, Lars and her younger brother Hans. Her father, Professor Lars Anderssen, was an eminent scientist and had secured a position at a nearby university. Brockford was certainly not a student town, but was within commuting distance of the University and so attractive for staff looking for a quieter place in which to live. She noticed Jim in the classroom almost immediately; he was a bit of a loner, tall with dark hair and he somehow seemed distanced from the rest of the pupils, sort of aloof but in the sense that he didn't really belong. Her cultural background and striking looks made her feel like an outsider too. She discovered that he was intelligent and mature for his age. They joined forces, so to speak, and became such close friends that people rarely saw them apart. Somehow, their union meant that they were included more and became part of a wider group of friends. However, although most people thought it inevitable, they were never a couple in the romantic sense. She often wondered why; maybe neither wanted to make the first move, maybe a friendship such as theirs was too precious to risk incurring damage from the stress of a physical relationship, maybe the time just wasn't right…maybe Jim just didn't see her in that way…whatever it was, it just never happened. She had a tough time when she first moved away from her family and friends; she didn't enjoy her chosen degree course as much as she thought she would and she had trouble adapting to a different town. Not wanting to disappoint anyone, she just got on with it and years passed by in a blur. She heard about Jim's progress through her father, and was glad that he had done well for himself. A good job in London, a nice modern apartment; he had kept his looks too, she had learnt from a mutual acquaintance…no point in getting in contact, why would he want to meet up with someone from the past? Now, she thought, he seemed different, sort of vulnerable, but she couldn't identify what made her feel that way.

*

Jim and Nova sat by the counter and reminisced about the time they spent together as teenagers. Behind the Swimmer house, there is an overgrown path that leads through the woods to a small ridge, which is largely unspoilt and well sheltered. This was locally called Badger Ridge, although it is not named as such on any maps. A group from school used to meet there now and then, bearing in mind that this was a time before mobile phones and when eating out was a rare treat. It was strange how youngsters nowadays met at local cafes and were dependent on Wi-Fi connections. Along with Jim and Nova, this group often included Sarah Swimmer, as she was then, and a few of her friends, as well as Jason, Michael and Thomas McDougall, Julian Green, and young Hans- although his tender age meant that he was mostly considered a nuisance by the others.

However, those years were also marked by loss. The Anderssen family had only been in town for a couple of years when the unthinkable happened; Anna Anderssen became ill and was shortly after diagnosed as suffering from ovarian cancer. Jim was there for Nova, as a listening ear and a practical help, and she and Hans also began to spend more time at the Swimmer house during this time. Nova lost her mother a few months before her 16th birthday, and the Professor was barely able to get up each day, such was his grief. Hans was sent, temporarily, to live with his mother's sister in Norway but never returned to Brockford for more than a brief visit. Nova remained at home and gradually her father's mood improved, although he was never the same again. Nova and her father started to spend a lot of time at the Swimmer's house. While the adults talked late into the evening Jim and Nova grew ever closer. They listened to music, discussed books and films and- to a lesser extent- worked on their homework together. Neither had found that connection with anyone else, and both were now single and heading towards their mid-forties. Those few years and the memories associated with them were inevitably marked with sadness, but now that they were so much older and had lived so many years apart they could both see how precious they were.

Nova apologised that she had not been in touch following the death of Jim's parents. She had been abroad and had heard the news belatedly; she confessed that she started to write a letter of consolation, but just couldn't seem to find the right words, and then she had found out about her father's illness and, well, everything just seemed to happen all at once. She was always pragmatic and, remembering Jim's sensitive nature, felt she should say something.

'Losing your parents is hard, whatever the circumstances. But, people live and people die; those left behind must find a way to move on. You only get one life; don't waste it,' Nova said, looking straight into Jim's eyes,

Jim returned her gaze, and felt an impulse which compelled him to ask Nova out for a dinner date on Friday night, at Caligari's, where they reputedly served the best pizza in Brockford. He used the word dinner date; did she realise what he meant? Nova asked for a rain check, but stressed that it was because she was committed to caring for her father in the evenings and placed a hand over his reassuringly to confirm that she wasn't making an excuse. She said that she was on her own in the bookshop this week, but that she would be free for lunch any day next week.

'It's not forever,' she said. 'But Dad is in a bad way and the carers only come in during the day.'

Jim understood and said that he was grateful for any time she could spare and was rewarded with a thankful smile a warm hug.

A small group of customers had assembled in the shop, so Jim thought that he should take his leave before he became an encumbrance. He left his mobile number with Nova, and then also scribbled down the home telephone number just in case there was an issue with the mobile phone network. Jim promised to meet Nova at one o clock the following Monday, but invited her to call at any time if she felt like a chat or needed anything. As he looked back at Nova through the shop window, he noticed that she was wearing gaudy pumpkin earrings but, in his eyes, she had hardly changed since they were awkward teenagers. Just a little older; like Jim she had gained a few more lines and a couple of extra pounds. Her hair was a darker blonde, maybe, and she looked pale and tired, just as she had when her mother was ill. Her accent had changed a little, and Jim started to wonder what she had been doing in the years that they were apart, where had she been, who...then he stopped and checked himself, mid thought.

What did it matter? He finally understood that she was the only woman he had ever cared for and the one that no other could compare to, no matter what allowances he made.

'I am an idiot,' Jim said to himself. 'A bloody idiot and a coward. And I need to grow up and stop wasting time, take a few risks now and then. What's the worst that could happen?'

Jim had started to realise that he looked back so fondly on Brockford and the family home because he associated both with Nova. He was overly fond of his parents but Nova Anderssen was the one person who made everything better than it really was.

The rest of the day went by very slowly, with Jim thinking that it was a long time until he would see Nova next to follow up on their conversation. Next week! He thought about popping into the shop when it was quiet, or sending some flowers as a gesture, but he didn't want to put her under pressure. He decided a couple of friendly text messages would suffice, and once sent he would wait anxiously for a reply, like a lovesick teenager. Jim was relieved when darkness came; a light appeared in the summer house window so he eagerly made his way down the garden pathway to play a game of chess with Walter, who also distracted him with tales of his neighbours and their secret habits. He told Walter that his first shift as a taxi driver was the following day, and this caused some amusement with Walter telling tales of some of the cars that his father had bought over the years. Jim remembered that he never wore a seatbelt as a child, and neither did his parents. He also remembered that, many years ago, a young friend of his had been seriously injured when he was flung through the windscreen from the back seat as he slept. It was later revealed that the boy's father has been drinking heavily at a party, and this memory always prevented Jim from idealising the small-town freedom and attitudes that prevailed when he was a youngster, where the provincial policeman was as guilty as the locals of drinking illegally after licencing hours and driving home regardless. Soon he would be responsible for the safety of others in his vehicle and he wasn't sure about how he felt about this. Walter reminded him that he was an experienced and careful driver, and that it was unlikely that he would be required to go any further than the airport, and that it was also his move. Jim could sense that his opponent was keen to claim victory, and forfeited the game, explaining why he would lose and speculating as to where he had made the fatal error. His chess skill had improved considerably, and Jim felt satisfied despite his loss as he bade Walter farewell and retired to the main house.

6
FIRST DAY

As Jim carefully parked his dark grey Prius outside Odin's Cars only premises, he was relieved to see that Thomas was waiting as agreed. Jim was grateful for the distraction, as his new and unlikely boss gave him a guided tour and instructions on the process of job allocation and acceptance and so on. He was introduced to the permanent drivers, but immediately forgot their names as he wasn't really paying attention. This was unlike Jim, who usually absorbed and retained detailed information easily, but he was preoccupied by his previous conversation with Nova. Was she trying to let him down gently? That wasn't her style, but she might have changed. No, he was sure that there wasn't a misunderstanding. The way she had reassuringly looked directly into his eyes and squeezed his hand as she made her excuses meant that she was sincere, and he knew that he would have to be patient and not fixate on every little sign or potential subtext.

Jim Swimmer was an eternal spectator, always preferring to observe rather than participate. For example, he wasn't an avid skier but he liked to go on skiing trips just to be in the mountains and look at the snow, to watch people falling over and showing off and generally being human. This meant that he had a keen eye for detail and he could often 'read' people better than their closest friends and family. He could almost always sense when someone was lying or was concealing a secret and could often anticipate what people would say next. Julian joked that Jim would be a much better police officer than him, and other people had said similar things. It was rather irritating when he was expected to recall conversations or events like a performer or as an adjudicator, especially as he wasn't one for the limelight. The exception to this was when Jim was too close, or too emotionally invested. In these cases, Jim was exceptionally short sighted and therefore he subconsciously tended to avoid close relationships; feeling uncertain and not in control was not something he liked. When he was a student of literature he preferred to study theoretical approaches or subtexts rather than face a text unfiltered. Maybe that was what he liked about postmodernism; the distance it created, the unreliable narrator, the awareness and even appreciation of artifice...Why was he thinking about this now? It was because Thomas had just asked him what he was currently reading.

Jim returned to the present time and looked at Thomas, who seemed to be sweating slightly despite the inclement weather and inadequate heating in the makeshift office, which was little more than a portacabin.

'Erm, I have a few books on the go right now,' Jim responded, unnerved at having been put on the spot. 'I am re-reading a couple of classics, and I finally got around to reading Knausgaard as well; tried to avoid him for ages due to all the hype but I am now halfway through the second book of the series and finding it hard to put down. I like his raw honesty and the writing is excellent, even in translation. Have you read them yet? Nova has them in the shop.'

Thomas's response was surprising, he became red in the face and began accusing the Norwegian author of being disreputable and disloyal, selling out his family for his own personal gain, calling him a talentless hack and declaring that he would never consider reading such a travesty...Jim was embarrassed by Thomas's outburst, although he wasn't sure why he should be, but was saved by the bell, so to speak, when his first job came in and he quickly departed for his first ever fare.

As he drove away, Thomas smiled and wished him luck, tapping the roof of the car in a friendly manner; a complete contrast with the irate and easily riled person Jim had just observed. They had never been particularly close friends, so Jim could not say whether this volatility was a new trait but he knew that he would have to tread carefully and try not to antagonise Thomas McDougall, at least while he was in his employ. His family was clearly a sensitive topic and one to avoid if possible.

The first fare was a simple pick up from the hospital to the customer's home. The second was a supermarket run. Then things started to get interesting. Julian had clearly told people about his aspiring career as an author of detective fiction, and in some people's minds that made him an amateur sleuth.

'Only in Brockford,' he thought.

It began with a simple missing cat, which was a serious issue for Lara's owner, Susan, who was elderly and obviously visually impaired. Jim promised to keep an eye open on his travels and agreed that he would create a few flyers, which meant waiting outside the customer's house while she went inside to find a photograph. Jim didn't dare accept Susan's offer to go inside for a cup of tea as he feared it would be some considerable time before she would allow him to leave in good conscience. It was his first day, after all. Although it was just a casual position and not a job that he really needed to keep for any length of time he still felt that he owed it to Thomas to take it seriously. As he stood waiting by the car, he noticed a thin grey-haired man watching him from a neighbouring garden, partially concealed behind a tall manicured hedge. Jim nodded and tried to wave in a discreet but friendly manner, but felt that he must have failed as the man just glared at him and then quickly moved away. Luckily, Susan appeared in her porch with some photographs and contact details. Jim walked briskly to the front door to save her unsteadily making her way along the path, and reassured her that he was happy to use his own email address on the flyer, in case anyone should have any general information concerning Lara's recent movements. It would take him ten minutes at most and he knew that there was a Brockford page on a social media site where he could also post a copy of the flyer. This would probably be more effective than a printed A4 poster, laminated and nailed to a tree, but Jim could see that the act of doing something was important to Susan, and so he promised to be in touch if he heard anything and moved on to the next job. The next job was to pick up someone called Derek, who was annoyed that the police were unable to help him find out who had knocked him off his bicycle at a junction the previous week. He wasn't badly hurt, but that wasn't the point, Derek explained; it was a hit and run, the driver was at fault but didn't stop.

'If you hear anything, you know, being in your line of work and doing the driving now, too. My family depend on me. I don't get sick pay, you know. It is the second time that I have been knocked off in as many months, and I am good on the roads…I will leave you my card,' Derek continued.

Jim truly wondered what he meant when he referred to his 'line of work.' He sympathised, but wasn't sure how he could help. A few more standard jobs ensued, then a comparatively young couple wanted to talk about a recent burglary at their home, where a small amount of money, electrical goods and some sentimental jewellery was taken. As the intruder was clearly no longer on the premises, it was several hours before the police attended, and they didn't express any expectation of apprehending the person or persons responsible.

Later another customer, a young mother, wanted to talk about recent vandalism in the street where she had lived for many years. She spoke without pausing for breath.

'It's the government, you know,' she said. 'They have a matrix, you see; the local police don't have a say about which crimes they investigate…it's not that they don't care. I get that. And it probably is just kids, there isn't much for them to do around here. But this sort of thing spirals out of control if it isn't nipped in the bud. I don't want them to get into trouble or nothing, I mean I was young once, not that long ago, eh, but we always knew where to draw the line. No respect, I suppose, but that's no excuse.'

Jim sympathised, empathised but ultimately didn't see what he could do even if, in some miraculous feat, he discovered the culprits. He had always had difficulty in saying no, so as a compromise he pulled out the leather-bound notebook that he had reserved for taking notes for the Maitland Green book and made a point of asking a few pertinent questions and carefully taking down the answers. During his next break, he picked up a flat white coffee in a takeaway cup and sat in his car, noting down all that customers had said to him. By the end of the day he had also added to his notebook several items of varying value taken from outside several properties in broad daylight, a taxi driver running a red light and a mysteriously broken window.

Jim was glad that he could sign off when he wanted, without any need to speak to Thomas directly. Now that he had completed his first day it was just a matter of working when he wanted to, and he had already planned to work mostly evenings and nights, when it would be quieter. He arrived home and put some leftovers in the microwave, which he then ate while creating the flyer and posting a scaled down version of this on the Brockford Local social media page. This took less than the projected ten minutes, so Jim went upstairs for a shower and to change his clothes. Feeling refreshed, he decided that he was in the mood for a glass of wine and that he would retire to the study to do a bit of writing while he was feeling amenable. He had started adapting the study into a suitable writing room, so he really ought to make use of it. However, he had only just taken the wine from the fridge in the kitchen when he noticed several notifications on the screen of his laptop computer, which he had left open on the old oak table. Maybe using his own details hadn't been such a good idea. Several private messages had appeared in his inbox, as well as a few comments underneath the post he had created less than an hour previously. Only two or three related to Lara the cat, and the remainder were about minor crimes he might like to investigate, or contained follow up information from the people he had spoken to earlier. 'Who do they think I am, Jessica bloody Fletcher?!' Jim thought to himself, then laughed at the absurdity of the situation. He would be having a chat with Julian, who was proving to be a good and loyal friend but also a tad indiscreet. First, though, he would need to speak to Walter, who must have arrived while he was upstairs as there was no light on in the summer house earlier. Although there was a path leading from the back gate directly to the summer house, Jim couldn't envisage Walter sitting in the dark for no good reason. Over a couple of very average games of chess, Jim explained the situation to his older friend, who found this state of affairs entertaining and asked if he knew why he always ended up with odd socks- that was a mystery worth solving, after all. Jim said he would sleep on it and said goodnight.

7
FIRST DATE

On Thursday Professor Anderssen was looking through a box of old photographs when he came across a grainy black and white picture, taken by his son Hans when he was young and developing an interest in photography. That was long before digital cameras, he recalled, when photography was less accessible and pictures were typically printed from film in the local chemist shop. With Anna's encouragement, he and Hans had converted the old pantry into a makeshift darkroom, where images were developed using odorous chemicals and hung up with pegs to dry. Hans was artistic and this proved to be an excellent way to combine science with a creative art. He looked at the picture for a long time. It was taken in the Swimmer's garden one summer: Sylvie was standing with her hand on John's shoulder, holding a wine bottle in a kind of wicker carafe and smiling at the camera, while John was seated, holding a glass slightly raised, looking somehow self-conscious. And there he was, on the left-hand side, dressed in his trademark slightly eccentric garb and watching his Anna who looked impeccable in a summer dress and was fussing a small dog which was settled on her lap. He couldn't recall the dog's name, or where it had come from, but he could remember that day, that last summer before he became a widow. Of all the people in the photograph, Professor Anderssen was now the last one standing, wishing that his scientist's brain would allow him to believe in an afterlife so that he might be reunited with his beloved Anna. He would sometimes wake at night, having dreamt that Heaven did exist after all but that he had been turned away as a lifelong atheist. Other times he would dream that they were reunited, but that she, being blonde and beautiful as she was shortly before she passed, either did not recognise her now elderly husband or was repulsed by his aging. Being a private man, he never mentioned these dreams to anyone. He thought maybe the medications were influencing his mind, or maybe he was showing signs of senility. Sometimes he woke up in the morning unsure of where he was and of what day it was, how old he was…he would lay there for sometimes thirty minutes or more, before he thought to check his watch or look at a calendar. Feeling his thoughts drifting in a direction that he didn't like, he picked up another photograph, noticing that his hands were unsteady and his skin paper thin as he did so. It was another of Han's photographs, taken the same day. He saw Sarah Swimmer, or Johnson as she now was, if he recalled correctly, posing in the foreground with her head to one side and her hands on her hips, and behind her were Jim and Nova, totally engrossed in whatever they were looking at, paying no attention to the camera. Jim with his slightly too long hair and Nova with slightly too much make up on; it was the eighties after all. But they looked so comfortable together, and Jim had been there for Nova when she lost her mother, when her own father was too engrossed in his own feelings of loss to properly take care of his own children. Nova and Jim. He remembered how they were always a package deal; everyone thought they would end up growing old together -they sometimes finished each other's sentences, and they often spoke the same words at the same time- but they somehow drifted apart as they became adults. The Professor sometimes thought that he was instrumental in their separation, for he had encouraged his daughter to spread her wings, to go out into the wider world and find her independence. He recalled that he had overheard Nova talking to a friend, just yesterday, saying that Jim was in town and had asked her out, and that she had wanted to go, but had declined. He had wanted his children to be independent and make their own choices but maybe it was time for the free-thinking father to interfere, he thought. It was not something he had done before, but he could feel time slipping away and what was the worst that could happen? He looked at the photograph again, and recognised that the way Jim looked at Nova was the same way that he looked at Anna. The professor reached forward carefully and picked up the telephone receiver, breathing heavily as he did so, preparing himself to make a couple of calls.

At eight thirty the following morning Jim received an unexpected text message from Nova. It seemed that her father had heard about Jim's dinner invitation and taken it upon himself to insist that she went, if it wasn't too late, bearing in mind that it was Friday today. He had even arranged for a local volunteer to sit with him early in the evening, and for an additional carer to pop in after that- and this was not something that the Professor, who was particularly private and fond of his own space, would usually do willingly. Nova sensed that he was pre-empting any objections that she might have and mitigating them before they could be validated.

'You must go,' he said, 'I know how much you love pizza.'

It was true that she was becoming tired of what the Professor called 'fusion' but what she considered to be a peculiar amalgamation of Nordic and 'older person' food. She had once been presented with gravlax accompanied by Yorkshire puddings, and he was very particular when she took the time to make a meal for them both. A glass or two of chilled white wine and some good company would also be more than welcome…

Jim was delighted and wasted no time as he carried his laptop into the kitchen and sat down at the table. He typed in his password- Nova23, as always. The message had suggested meeting at seven o clock, and so he thought he would book a table at Caligari's for seven thirty, to be safe. It was a Friday night so a reservation was probably necessary, and Jim didn't want to take any chances. It took only a few seconds to complete the online process; he hovered over the 'special requirements' box and contemplated requesting a window seat, or a table in a quiet corner, or maybe just not the table near the toilets or by the draughty front door. However, he could appreciate that this was a short notice booking, so he just clicked 'reserve table now' and then stared at his phone for the 30 seconds it took for the text confirmation to arrive.

Jim tapped his fingers on the oak table and felt guilty about his desire to replace it with something more modern. Initially, he had thought that moving back to his parent's rather old-fashioned house would be a novelty, and that he wouldn't want to change anything at all. However, now that he had settled in properly he started to notice more and more things that needed updating. General décor, security, furniture…he felt that the house was somehow aging him and he felt uneasy about this. Like owners who start to resemble their dogs, he felt that the house was starting to own him and he was taking on the old, worn out look and personality of the house. He was aware of the contradiction. On one hand, he was wallowing in the past and attaching too much importance to how his parents had arranged the house. On the other, he had implemented his Smart devices and had planned to extend his set up. By his own admission, he was incapable of living without technology. Nova had laughed when he explained that, when he first arrived, he kept talking to the house but got no response; he described how his London flat was filled with smart voice activated technology and sensors, and that simply recalling the habitual action of flicking a light switch had been a learning curve for him.

'It is ultimately just laziness- there needs to be a balance,' she told him, but she was still interested in how it all worked and could see many of the benefits.

Jim knew she was right, but didn't intend on changing his ways. In fact, he subsequently ordered several additional smart lightbulbs and hoped the Wi-Fi wouldn't go down anytime soon.

At five minutes to seven Jim found himself at the gate to Nova's house, holding a discreet bunch of pink roses and a bottle of Professor Anderssen's favourite liqueur. He thought it was too early to knock and was also questioning his choice of gift, given the circumstances, but then a young man who looked to be in his early twenties, appeared behind him. He was casually dressed and bore an exaggerated smile

'You must be Jim,' he said. 'Adam', he continued, offering his hand. 'Here to sit with the Professor for a couple of hours. Come on, the doors open.'

Jim followed Adam, who had a confidence that he both envied and was slightly irked by. It was the first time that he had seen the Professor in some time, and he barely recognised him. If it weren't for the distinctive blue eyes and the quirky dress sense he might have been a stranger. While Adam went to make coffee, Jim proffered his gift, mumbling that he wasn't sure if it was appropriate but that he knew it used to be a favourite tipple. The professor stopped him mid-sentence, smiled and said that he would keep it for a special occasion. They quickly caught up with the latest news and gossip, and just when there was nothing left to say Nova appeared in the doorway and said they should get going- thereby circumventing any potential awkward silences.

Nova hadn't had a reason to dress up lately, and as she walked with Jim, unsteadily in unfamiliar shoes, she expressed her fear that she might be overdressed and would look a little odd if everyone else in Caligari's was wearing jeans and warm clothes. It was the day before Guy Fawkes Night, and some of the local displays had been arranged over the next few days to avoid clashes and maximise attendances. The weather, although cold, was also dry with very little wind and the uniquely autumnal smell of bonfires and gunpowder hung in the air. Every few seconds a flash of lights appeared in the sky, accompanied by sudden loud noises. Jim reassured her that she looked amazing, as always, and most people would be having parties at home anyway. Despite Jim's reassurances, Nova still felt self-conscious and was relieved to arrive at the restaurant and be seated in a quiet corner where, without prompting, she immediately ordered a large glass of white wine. Realising how that might appear, she quickly added a justification.

'It has been a tough week so far- and it's not over yet.'

Jim smiled. He was planning on going all out, ordering champagne, but thought he would follow Nova's lead.

'Make that two glasses,' he added. 'And some olives. Thank you.'

He detested olives, but Nova used to like them, he recalled.

Nova quickly gave the latest update on her father's health, confirming Jim's understanding that only palliative care was an option. She then declared that she wanted an evening off, talking wasn't going to change anything and they managed to pass an enjoyable evening, with much reminiscing and laughter. Jim talked about the antics of his two nieces. He was particularly fond of his elder niece, Oli- short for Olivia- who could be described as a free-spirited tomboy who took great delight in challenging her mother's expectations. Evie, his other niece, was quiet and studious, unsure of what she wanted from life, but would no doubt find her place in due course. Jim also told light hearted stories about his recently divorced sister's disastrous re-entry into the world of dating. It was all done via apps nowadays, but she could never remember whether to swipe left or right, and didn't know the difference between Tinder and Grindr and Hinge.

'Sounds like a firm of solicitors to me, if I'm honest!' Nova observed.

Nova talked about her brother Hans, who she had been in regular contact with since her father's illness, and about some of the strange customers that came into the book shop with equally peculiar requests. They laughed about Jim's role as the 'reluctant amateur detective' and his overdependence on technology. The pizza was as good as they remembered, maybe even better, and at ten thirty, realising that they were the only ones left in the restaurant, Jim recommended that they let the staff go home and suggested a nightcap or coffee at his house. Nova, however, felt that she should get back to check on her father so Jim walked her home, and by the time they reached the front gate they had arranged a brief lunchtime meeting for the following day and self-consciously sealed the deal with a goodnight kiss; their first.

'So', Nova asked. 'Are we officially a courting couple?'

Jim nodded, smiling, and replied nervously.

'Well, after all these years it seems we finally are!'

*

At just after eleven o clock, Jim had arrived home, euphoric and feeling like he would never be tired again. He walked into the kitchen and put the house keys down on the worktop, beside the stove. He saw a light on in the summerhouse at the end of the garden, and impulsively picked up a bottle of brandy and two crystal glasses and walked cautiously, as always, along the path. Walter declined the drink that he offered, and explained that he was replaying an old game from memory, as best he could, before looking up and immediately noticing something different about Jim Swimmer.

'It went well with your lady friend, then. Your father always said you two belonged together, and that one day you would see it.'

Jim was surprised at this comment, as the whole evening had been a last-minute affair that he had not discussed with anyone. As if reading his mind, Walter continued.

'Not much gets past me in this town!'

Luckily, Jim had a late shift the following day, although it only took forty-five minutes for Walter to corner his opponent's King in a classic endgame strategy.

As Jim drew the curtains in the bedroom, he heard a noise outside and felt uneasy; it couldn't be Walter as he had already left. The window faced the street outside but as the house was located at the far end of a cul-de-sac it was usually very quiet, with no through traffic. Last night, however, he was woken twice when his car alarm was inexplicably triggered. He had attributed that to the wind, or maybe falling twigs, or even a fox. Not for the first time, Jim had a sense that he was being watched, but he soon dismissed such foolish thoughts as a cat darted out from behind the hedge and ran across the road before disappearing into a neighbouring garden. This reminded Jim that he had located Susan's missing cat. A family in the next town had found Lara hiding in their shed, and had been feeding and caring for her as she had no collar or means of identification. The family could provide confirmation of a scar that developed following an operation a few years ago, and so Jim agreed to collect the cat and reunite her with her rightful owner before he went to work the following day.

'First case closed,' he muttered to himself..

8
BERGMAN COMES TO TOWN

Brockford Independent Picture House had operated on the outskirts of the town for many years, although Jim did sometimes wonder how they managed to keep going when the new, larger cinema had opened in the town centre. He concluded that it must rely on students, special events and charitable donations. Walter had talked about *The Seventh Seal* the night before, mentioning that it was being shown as part of a Bergman season, and Jim knew immediately that Nova would want to see at least one of the films on show, even though she probably had the entire collection on DVD. Thinking it would be a nice gesture to go ahead and make a booking, he went into the study- which was now his own private sanctuary- and took his laptop out of the drawer and placed it on the desk in front of him. He had decided to use the extra money that he earned from driving to invest in a large screen all in one PC, but he hadn't quite got around to organising this yet. He had, however, successfully installed his trusty 'Reverb' Smart Home Hub and linked this to the wireless bridge concealed in the cupboard under the stairs, and therefore could control the lighting.

'Holly- Study lights- one hundred per cent,' he said aloud and the lighting adjusted seamlessly, accompanied by a friendly 'Ok'.

He asked 'Holly' to update him on the latest news and weather reports, while he looked up the film listings online. *Smiles of a Summer Night* jumped out at him as being a good option, after all it was described as a comedy, not something usually associated with Bergman. Although the settings for some of the other options were quite stunning and would appeal to Nova, the subject matter was rather serious and gloomy. Maybe it wasn't the right time for too much existential angst, with all that was happening with the Professor right now. It was only showing that night, but he wanted to spend quality time alone with Nova again and, not being ready to expose his emotions or wanting to appear too keen, he felt that he needed a valid reason to take her away from the Professor for the evening. A quick sandwich and a thirty-minute walk through the park just wasn't enough. He went through the online booking procedure, saying aloud to 'Holly' that it was about time she learnt a few new skills so that he wouldn't have to complete these forms, although most of the fields were automatically filled anyway.

Jim then left to collect the wandering cat. Thomas had called earlier to ask Jim if he would be able to change his shift and do a couple of hours mid-morning as one of the regular drivers was unexpectedly absent; he had agreed so he would have to amend his schedule slightly. This all went to plan, and Susan was overjoyed when he dropped off the pet carrier containing her beloved cat, and Jim made a point of waving and saying a cheery 'good morning' to her nosy male neighbour as he returned to his car.

In the event, Nova had to reluctantly decline the invitation to the cinema as she was unable to find cover at short notice. He called her from the taxi office later that morning, and the conversation was overheard by Thomas.

'So, you have a spare ticket? I am partial to a bit of Swedish cinema myself, I wouldn't mind tagging along if you are short on company…'

Although a night with his moody employer didn't exactly appeal to Jim, he couldn't think of an acceptable excuse on the spot. He later thought he could have offered both tickets to Thomas; maybe he could set up a proper date with someone, as he was known to be a confirmed bachelor.

'If you are driving, you can pick me up on the way- about seven o clock. It's a date!' Thomas declared.

Jim was feeling relieved that Thomas didn't insist on dinner or drinks first.

'We can grab a bite to eat afterwards. My treat!' added Thomas as Jim walked out to the car, ready for his first fare of the day.

When he told Nova later, during their rushed lunchtime rendezvous, she had laughed and joked that they made a lovely couple. Jim remembered that smile from all those years ago; the same smile. It is enough, for now, he decided. He would spend all the time he could with Nova, but any time she could spare for him right now was sufficient. It would have to be.

*

Jim decided against getting changed for his evening with Thomas, he didn't want to give him the wrong idea and indicate that it was something that might be repeated on a regular basis. Thomas on the other hand had clearly dressed to impress, and was wearing what looked like a newly bought shirt and was drenched with an excess of expensive aftershave. Thomas seemed genuinely excited to be going out on the town, and Jim felt guilty, immediately resolving to make to make more of an effort to be friendly towards the man that he had considered to be his employer first and acquaintance second. It was a bit strange, but he had never really considered him to be a friend, even though he was part of the group that used to meet up when they were teenagers. Thomas's twin brother, Jason, was a bit of a lad, always up to something shady and you wouldn't have taken them for twins. It wasn't just that they weren't identical; they were very different in height, appearance and personality. He also seemed a lot older, and always associated with the sort of people that made Jim nervous. When he started the taxi business with Thomas there was a bit of talk about his motives and when he vanished from Brockford many years ago, there were rumours that he had been given a hefty prison sentence for some sort of serious misdemeanour. Nothing appeared in the local papers, so Jim took the gossip with a pinch of salt although it would not have surprised him if the rumours were proved to have a solid base. Thomas's younger brother, Michael or Mikey as he was often called, was the same age as Jim and was much more likeable; sharp witted, quick and extraordinarily cheeky. He was popular with the girls and had twinkling blue eyes and curly dark hair that he had inherited from his Irish grandfather. It must be said that Mikey always made you laugh, and Jason was a dark horse but he was loyal to a fault and would stick up for his friends no matter what. He was someone that you would want on your side, and you would never dare to cross him, and as a result you would not want to upset his brothers. Jim only had classes with Michael but the brothers came as a package deal. Yet try as he might he couldn't recall much of any consequence about Thomas. He couldn't remember what music he liked, what TV programmes he preferred, or anything specific about him. He seemed quite volatile and prone to over-reaction nowadays, but this was not a trait that Jim would have associated with him in the past. It had transpired, through a conversation with one of his colleagues that he had met outside the coffee shop, that only the previous day Thomas had a vicious row with Harry, the absentee taxi driver, and he was now trying to repair the damage and persuade him to return to work. It was something and nothing, apparently, but it had all been blown out of proportion very quickly and it wasn't the first time this sort of thing had happened. Jim found it hard to imagine anyone falling out with 'Happy Harry', as he was affectionately known. He was possibly the most easy- going person in Brockford; a genuinely nice guy who would do anything for anyone. Maybe Thomas felt frustrated about being the only one of the brothers left in town; left behind when they moved on to better things. Regardless, Thomas was amenable enough now and couldn't be more charming although Jim recoiled slightly without thinking as Thomas's moist, clammy hand met his during an unnecessarily formal handshake.

Jim was relieved that they were running later than planned, as they entered the auditorium and the film began almost immediately. This negated the need for awkward small talk in the first instance. Before the lights went completely dark Jim looked around and saw how out of place they looked among the middle-aged couples, the lone people dressed in dark clothes, the scattering of university students… Jim wished that he was at home sitting in front of his computer. Since he had tied up so much of his time, he had experienced a strong impulse to write and he had told Thomas on the way to the cinema that he wouldn't be working for a few days, as was their casual agreement, but would happily cover some of the less popular shifts later in the week. Thomas said that he was happy with this arrangement, as he had managed to resolve the issue with the errant driver, and theirs was a flexible arrangement, after all. The film dragged by, and Jim realised that classic Swedish cinema wasn't quite as he remembered it; it appeared dated somehow, not quite as relevant as he had thought. He resisted the urge to take his phone out to check his messages, although he was sorely tempted, and he silently chastised himself for having such a poor attention span. At last, the film ended and they both escaped the confines of the stuffy auditorium. It was 5 November, and the sound of fireworks exploding filtered in from all directions, lighting up the sky with intermittent flashes of colour and smoke. Jim had gone outside alone and was waiting by the car for Thomas, who had gone back inside to retrieve his coat from the cloakroom, when he heard a loud noise resembling a gunshot echo across the carpark. He thought it must be a firework gone astray and gave it no further consideration. Jim was lost in thought, contemplating a possible story arc for Maitland Green when Thomas arrived a couple of minutes later, looking a bit pale and making his excuses for wanting to go directly home.

'Bit of an upset stomach,' he explained.

Jim tried to not let his relief look too obvious. It is one thing to try to get along with someone, but the effort this required was often immense, while the rewards were scant. Thomas had this way of looking at people as they spoke, as if he were interpreting their words into another language, Jim thought, or maybe it was a look of disgust, no, more of disapproval. Regardless, he was glad to be home alone with a few hours to spare. After sending a text message to Nova he tipped a large bag of salted kettle chips in a bowl and poured himself an extra-large glass of crisp chardonnay, and then spent the rest of the evening with his feet up on the heavily padded leather sofa, making disorderly notes in his untidy scrawl while half watching a crime and mystery channel, which was peppered with more advertisements than he could believe were permissible. This was why he rarely watched live television, he thought, but he still left it on until he went to bed around midnight.

.

9
THE BROCKFORD FILE

Using his recent experiences as inspiration, Jim decided to use his free Sunday morning to start work on the first Maitland Green book. He initially worked quickly, creating two draft chapters in a short space of time, but when he read through them he noticed inconsistencies and outright contradictions, so he began making notes on characters and a created a basic timeline in Excel to keep himself on track. This exercise took longer than the actual writing, but he persevered and at lunchtime he decided to see if Julian was free to come over and help him out. The characters were fine, but he needed some inspiration for plotlines, some ideas and background information about procedures and so on. Jim had just seen an email about a lunchtime pizza delivery deal so he could bribe his policeman ally with junk food and cold beer, if he wasn't working or tied up with the family. Jim sent him a text message and Julian replied that his wife had taken the children to a birthday party so he was at a loose end for a couple of hours and would come over shortly. In fact, he arrived at Jim's house in less than ten minutes and they quickly started work.

This was the first time that Jim had allowed another person into his study since he had customised it to suit himself. It was his haven; he felt secure ensconced with his books and his technology, but when he saw his private space through someone else's eyes he felt a little embarrassed. He could have moved everything into the kitchen, if he had thought about it in advance, but it was too late and he was obliged to demonstrate the voice activated technology, which included ordering the pizza, adjusting the heating, lights...unfortunately, he joked, he did not yet have a robot to bring in a beer from the fridge. Jim returned from the kitchen with a couple of bottles, just as Julian was asking Holly obscure questions, trying to 'catch her out'. Jim explained how he believed that smart homes are the future, despite people's reluctance. Imagine, he said, when you are older, possibly infirm and lacking in mobility, how technology could enable you to maintain your independence and privacy. Less reliance on other people, reduced costs…Julian argued for the ethical implications, of the lack of human contact and empathy…Jim responded with a counter argument about the inhuman treatment of the elderly by some human beings, and of how care workers are poorly paid, considered low skilled and not widely respected for the job they do…and from there they went on to discuss artificial intelligence and how, at school in the eighties, they would never have predicted how much of an impact technology would have on everyday life. Also, what happened to the flying cars everyone predicted? Technology will only ever really emulate empathy; they agreed on this one thing.

'Holly- can you feel?' Julian asked.

'I am not designed for that sort of thing,' the device replied.

'Not what I meant!' laughed Julian, just as the skinny pizza delivery agent- 'Colin the Conqueror', according to the live online tracker- arrived at the green front door.

As Jim reached for a second slice of pizza, he explained to Julian that he had been eating and drinking unhealthily of late and not getting much exercise. He cited the example of effectively having had crisps for dinner the previous day after getting back from the cinema. This comment made Julian stop in his tracks.

'The BIPH?' he asked, using the local term for the Brockford Independent Picture House. 'You mean you haven't heard what happened?'

Jim confirmed that he had heard nothing, so Julian continued.

'There was a shooting there last night; some kid was arrested at the scene, the victim is alive but unconscious and in a bad way, I believe. They will be looking for witnesses or anyone who was in the area yesterday evening. I will give you the lead investigator's details, even if you didn't see anything they will want to speak to you. First crime of this sort in Brockford for years, I reckon.'

Although Jim felt unnerved by this revelation, he didn't believe that the noise he heard was a gunshot and even if it was he didn't think that anything would have been achieved by his moving to investigate further. It appeared that the police had their man, and Jim was hopeless at first aid, so he would have just dialled 999 like any other person. While Julian looked over his shoulder, he looked up the local newspaper's website; a limited report plagued with typos, fundamental spelling mistakes and interspersed with screenshot padding from social media. Nothing of note to be found there. Julian pointed out an article about badgers in the woods behind the house, asking Jim if he had noticed the rare 'ginger' badger that had allegedly been spotted. He confirmed that he had not, although he intended to have a twilight walk and maybe take some photographs, when he could find the time. Julian said he would join him.

The two men swiftly decided to move on as time was limited. Jim asked for some advice about the content so far, and Julian explained his thoughts.

'The trick is, I believe, to not include anything that isn't relevant, that doesn't drive the plot forward. Focus on the facts. But at the same time, you need red herrings, to lead the reader astray before adding an unexpected twist. So, by that reasoning, the red herrings must link to some part of the plotline. That sounds a bit convoluted. Also, you need more human interest; you want characters that the reader will like and identify with- I mean, why would you choose to spend time with people you didn't care for? They don't have to be perfect as that would just be bland, boring…but there must be something to justify an emotional investment on the part of your reader.'

Jim knew what he was saying; writing for a modern audience needed to be economical. It wasn't that books needed to be dumbed down, he supposed, but most people didn't have the time nowadays to devote to huge, complex tomes. Time and effort were valuable resources; they needed something that could be dipped into during a lunch break or read on the tube. Chronological timelines and clearly segmented chapters were preferable, especially when reading on electronic devices. He wasn't writing War and Peace. Strict editing would be required, but for now he was concerned with the plot, mapping out the narrative. The study had large patio doors which opened out onto a small patio on the far side of the garden, with the woodland area showing through gaps in the boundary fence. Jim and Julian decided to use these glass doors as a 'crazy wall', using sticky notes and drawing pictures to illustrate connections and timelines. Jim had to admit that this visual aid was more effective than a spreadsheet for the bigger details, but did suggest that he might refer to it as an 'investigation wall', lest anyone should overhear them talking. Jim asked if they had interactive screens at the station, but Julian laughed and explained that they just had whiteboards, which were rarely used for investigative purposes. They both stared at what was in front of them; Jim thought that there was something missing.

'We need some red string or something,' he said. 'I have some blue tack and some old tinsel!'

Julian laughed again, but then pulled a serious face and replied.

'Now you are being silly- red string is for maps…I think. What you might find helpful, though is this notebook. I noted down details of a few cases I have dealt with over the years, or heard about from my older colleagues. I haven't used real names, for obvious reasons, and it is between us, but might give you some ideas. I'll have to be off in a minute, but have a look later and let me know if you have any questions. Oh, and careful how you open it; my son Robbie used to collect newspaper clippings about crimes and the police from the local paper, when he was younger and in his naivety thought that I was the only copper in town and solved every case- single handed, of course. He lost interest a long time ago and now wants to be a PE teacher or something like that. But I thought you might find some inspiration from them so I tucked them inside on the off chance. Just bin them if they aren't any use.'

Before Julian returned home to his family, Jim decided to ask him what he could remember about the young Thomas McDougall. Being the same age as Jim's elder sister Sarah, Julian recalled that he was at college whilst most of the group were still at school, so could only remember the McDougall brothers clearly in a social setting. He did however contradict Jim's version of what had happened to one of the absent brothers over the years. Jason was dead; he died several years ago when he was fatally injured in a car accident. It happened on a quiet country road in Scotland and so wasn't reported locally. Julian was aware of this as one of his colleagues was dispatched to inform the next of kin, who happened to be Thomas McDougall. Regarding Michael, Julian was unable to verify Jim's notion that he had moved away for work and settled down, although he had no reason to refute this either. He certainly wasn't in town when Jason had died. Thomas would have no obvious reason to lie, but then he would have no reason to obscure the truth about Jason's fate either. Fate was what Jim thought about lately, although it was never something that he sincerely believed in. He struggled with the thought that maybe, just maybe, it was fate that had brought him back to Brockford at the same time as Nova.

It was late on Sunday night when Jim finally shut down his laptop for the day. He would have kept writing, but his new twenty-seven inch all in one computer was arriving the next day, and he knew he would need to set it up before starting work. In the event, the delivery arrived shortly after nine o clock the following morning so he could get a substantial amount of work completed early in the day. Jim even had time to pop in to the local Police Station at lunchtime and provide details of his whereabouts on the evening of the shooting incident, for what it was worth. In the evening, he sat in his study with a glass of wine, listening to Chopin's Ballade No. 1 in G minor, Op. 23- his lucky number- and admiring the indulgent 5k screen where he could easily observe three pages of text at once. He put Julian's notebook, which he had mentally nicknamed *The Brockford File*, to one side and decided he would look through it at a later date. For now, he wanted to keep writing for as long as he could stay awake.

.

10

MEMORIES

Jim was up early the next day as his older sister Sarah was coming down to stay for the night, as agreed, to go through their parents' belongings and catch up with her younger brother. Jim asked Holly what day it was, and she kindly informed him that it was Tuesday 8 November; the US election day. He sighed, as he realised that Sarah would want to keep up to date with the developments, while he had so far managed to avoid most of the campaign shenanigans. The edited highlights were more than enough to let him know that it was a case of hoping that the American voters would opt for the lesser of two evils, and he had no influence in the result so he thought about other things. She wasn't bringing the children, so Jim went to the local supermarket to buy a couple of bottles of red wine; her favourite since her divorce, it seemed. It might be a long night. As he walked through the aisles he thought that maybe he should be making a bit more of an effort to entertain her, cook something nice, but he ultimately decided to buy some fresh artisan bread and a selection of cheese and cold meats for lunch, a few random snacks and he would then order a takeaway for supper. They would be busy; it would save time, he thought, as he justified this decision. Regardless, wasn't he taking time out to be here now, at the shops? Jim could have ordered supplies online and it would have been delivered to his house within a couple of hours, but he had dismissed that idea as soon as it materialised as he knew how particular Sarah could sometimes be. His sister, he thought, was so much more sophisticated than he was. She hosted dinner parties and had middle class aspirations. He didn't resent this as she had worked hard for everything that she achieved and had made a place for herself in her local community, but she sometimes felt like a stranger to him. It wasn't just the way she dressed or the way she spoke; she was different somehow. Although they kept in contact and maintained a genial relationship they had still grown apart over the years. Jim thought how different it was with Nova. When he reacquainted himself with his soul mate and they began a serious relationship he still saw the same girl; the same eyes, laugh and smile. She obviously looked older and had gained a little weight, but this suited her. She was as knowledgeable and well-read as always so they always had something to talk about, even if they didn't always agree. All those years wasted…

'Having a party?' the cashier asked abruptly, bringing Jim back into the present.

He smiled at the thought of buying alcohol at such an early hour of the day in a small town like Brockford. People might gossip, but he was not in the mood for making small talk with a stranger, so he simply mumbled a response.

'Something like that,' he said, and paid using the contactless app on his mobile phone before packing up his groceries and heading back to the Prius.

Arriving home, Jim made coffee and went into the sanctuary of his study for an hour, feeling more like himself as he typed another chapter describing in detail the adventures of Maitland Green. Maitland, he thought, you started out as a non-character, a cipher, but it seems you are developing into a much more complex character. Maitland's background, his backstory, had become more of a focus, and the world around him anchored him in time and place. A lot of changes were needed. Just as he typed the final sentence of the chapter there was a sharp knock at the door, so Jim quickly saved his progress and rose from his black leather chair, asking the ever-amenable Holly to mute the lighting as he did so.

Sarah had the foresight to bring various items with her; boxes, bin bags, labels, marker pens, folders for documents, as well as wine, food and an overnight bag. Jim thought that she had probably spent a lot more money on wine than he had. Considerably more.

'Talk about a time warp! I don't think this place has changed since I last lived here. Put the kettle on, Jim, then we can get started!' she said, giving him a quick hug then pushing him away while looking around the house at the same time.

There was something unusual about his sister today, he noticed; she was more like her old self. She was dressed informally, with minimal make up and was wearing old comfortable jeans and a well-worn, baggy jumper; she was eager to climb into the attic and begin lugging boxes around. It might be the absence of the children, Jim thought- today she was a sister rather than a mother. Perhaps it was being in the old family home with just her little brother, who she could boss around and tease, that had made her more casual, at ease. She chatted easily about everything and anything, urging Jim to update the house if he were intending to stay here.

'Knock down a few walls. Get rid of that awful wallpaper, much too dark and dated.'

Jim nodded and explained that his intention was to do as she had suggested, but he had wanted to get her approval first. As a courtesy.

'Nova will be over later, this evening. She is picking up some Chinese food on the way; be good to catch up!' Sarah said, casually, changing the subject without warning.

He hadn't mentioned their relationship developments to his sister, so was caught off guard. Noting his surprise, Sarah explained that, although not technically minded like her baby brother, she did use social media, and it wasn't just to keep tabs on her kids, she did use it to communicate with old friends too. After all, if she relied on Jim to keep her updated on all the news she would be hopelessly out of date. This was true, he supposed, and to be frank he was glad that everything was out in the open now. Despite his interest in technology and gadgets, Jim was not a particularly keen advocate of social media platforms and avoided these whenever possible. Jim had contacted Nova's brother, Hans, and often communicated with him via email so he made a point of letting Sarah know this. Hans seemed happy and had a successful career as a photographer, mixing artistic endeavours with event photography. It was hard to associate the insecure youngster with the older Hans, who came across as charming with a wicked sense of humour. And quite good looking too, Nova had said, although she might be biased in this matter.

They tried to organise a system. Clothes for charity and clothes to throw away. The same with ornaments, trinkets. Jim successfully persuaded Sarah to take the dinner set which had originally belonged to their grandparents. It was agreed that some of the photographs and collectables could be stored for now. It was all going well, but then Sarah decided that Jim should keep his mother's wedding and engagement rings, 'just in case.' He didn't think this was a good idea; Sarah had two daughters and it should stay in the family, he argued. The engagement ring was stunning in its simplicity, an art deco style diamond set design that was not the sort you saw in shops these days, and the matching wedding band was engraved with an unusual pattern. Sarah didn't think it was the sort of thing young people liked these days, and so Jim agreed that he would keep hold of it for now, just to enable them to make some progress as time was short.

Jim was especially pleased to clear out his parents' former bedroom, where he was sleeping each night. Although he had adapted the study to suit himself, he had deliberately left the rest of the house, overall, untouched. He had replaced the eiderdown with a duvet, removed the heavy dark curtains and installed a basic, modern blind. He had also moved a few things around and installed some of the smart home technology he had purchased, but that was pretty much it. He explained to Sarah that local charities had declined most of the furniture, as it was too bulky for modern houses and just wasn't popular these days. He could understand; Swedish designed flat-pack furniture was cheap and functional so why have a home that resembled a guest house from the 1950s? Sarah suggested storing some of the furniture in the garage as a short-term solution, and Jim couldn't believe that he hadn't thought of that himself. The garage was empty, as the family car had been disposed of some time ago.

'I'll get Julian to help me shift it later this week; Thomas is fine with me taking time out when I need it,' said Jim, realising too late that the mention of his employer would open the door to a discussion on his life choices, his lack of career; a mini lecture was surely imminent...

However, to Jim's surprise Sarah knew all about his writing project and was supportive, advising him to make the most of this time as such opportunities don't come along very often; she reminded him that you only get one chance at life and sometimes you just need to reassess where you are going and where your priorities lie...He suspected Nova's intervention as she had said virtually the same thing when they first got together but he remained silent and simply nodded in the right places.

It was the coldest day of the year so far. Jim had de-iced the car windows that morning and left the engine running. He was reminded of the cold mornings he experienced as a young child when he could feel the cold air on his face when he walked into school. It was a time when boys wore balaclavas over their faces- if you did that now you would probably be a suspected terrorist. Anyway, *he* always drew the line at a knitted hat. Surely, he was exaggerating? It couldn't have been that much colder. And then there was always a cool kid who never wore a proper coat, whatever the weather. Yes, it was a type of cold that you never seem to experience in London, hard to explain but nevertheless true. Maybe it was because no one ever stood still in the capital, except to queue. Initially, Jim thought that he would miss London more. Sometimes he yearned for the later shop opening times, when everything in Brockford was closed and he hadn't even thought about what time it was; sometimes he couldn't remember which day it was either.

He looked at his sister quizzically and asked her a random question.

'Do you remember those mittens you used to have, with the string attached so you couldn't lose them? I think Mum made them, they had a fair isle pattern around the cuffs.'

Lost in her thoughts, she turned around, stopped for a moment and laughed.

'God, yes, I had a matching jumper...no child over the age of five would be seen dead wearing those nowadays! Mind you, I think the jumpers might be coming back into fashion. Shall we drive into town and drop off some of these bags? We can take my car; its bigger and the seats go down easily.'

A trip into town took twice as much time as usual, with Sarah bumping into old friends and acquaintances and feeling obliged to enquire about their wellbeing, albeit briefly. As she talked to various people he could again see the adult side of Sarah coming to the fore, the way she spoke was more formal and careful, she held herself straight and accentuated every gesture, focussed on how well the children were progressing, how she had been improving her home, speculated about her next holiday abroad…They got home again eventually, made lunch and continued with their endeavour, making a good amount of progress which culminated with both of them agreeing that Jim could dispose of all that was left as he pleased and in his own time. A good day's work, he thought. By five o clock, only paperwork was left to sort through but Sarah convinced Jim that it would be better to leave this for another time when they could be more attentive.

The Professor had taken well to Adam, who was happy to keep him company at any time that he wasn't working. Adam always said that he was there 'to keep him company', never to care for him or to nurse or support, and maybe this was why they got on well. To be fair, the sharp-witted Professor Anderssen was always amenable and could get on with most people if he put his mind to it. Nova came over, as planned, and they all ate together and drank more wine than was usually permitted on a weekday evening. Well, the two women mostly drank and chatted while Jim watched, enjoying their gossip and thinking back to the old days, when things were so much more straightforward. Sarah insisted on eating with chopsticks, although she was hopeless with them, as it meant that she would eat less and more slowly and therefore not put on so much weight. She looked at Jim and suggested that he should try it, to which he responded with a query about how many calories were in red wine, offering to look it up, asking if would she prefer a smaller glass, maybe an egg cup. Jim liked to sit back and let them talk, but he interjected now and then, testing out some renovation ideas, and they mostly thought his plans were good, although they did laugh at his lack of clutter. What they called ornaments, he called dust catchers. He did concede that he might speak to Rosie about coming in to help more often with domestic chores, for he had underestimated the amount of work required to keep a house of this age and size in good order. He had invested in the ReverBot robot vacuum cleaner, a clever machine that would have worked well in an open plan residence but was not so efficient in a house like this; the layout provided too many obstacles. There were quite simply too many variables for the device to contend with, such as the numerous doors and accompanying raised thresholds, not to mention the thickness of the heavy carpets. Sarah took this opportunity to explain to Jim how much

Rosie had helped their parents in their final years, and he felt ashamed and foolish at not realising this. Had he just seen what he wanted to see, or what they wanted him to see? He should have done more to help them out, visited more often instead of prioritising his work schedules. Sensing his change of mood, Sarah swiftly steered the conversation in another direction and asked Nova if she had met Jim's new 'lady friend', Holly, and how she felt about having competition, which led to a good-natured teasing session. This ended with Jim trying to convince them that the house was haunted, using his mobile phone to make the living room lights flicker while he was in the kitchen pouring out more wine. When he returned to his guests he demonstrated the Smart Home set up that he had installed; as well as the Reverb Smart Home device, he had invested in several of the miniature versions, the Reverb Wedges. The little wedge shape devices were discreetly placed in corners but could pick up sound commands and link to speakers almost as well as the larger unit. Lighting, heating, domestic appliances, television, music could all be controlled via these little gizmos using voice commands once the wake word was spoken or, if the voice pattern was confirmed, it was possible to use one of the tiny remote controls scattered about the house. There was usually one to be found down the side of the armchair, Jim confessed, if ever one was needed. There was also the option of a mobile phone app if this was preferable and installed on the appropriate device and connected to the network. He demonstrated how he could add items to lists and how these updates were then send to him via email or text message, something he had set up himself. Nova used the voice control to put on some music, and explained how she found the constant electronic voice confirmation irritating, so Jim showed her how to mute this by turning the response sound down and then saved her voice pattern to the authorised user list.

'See,' Jim told her, quite seriously. 'Shows how much I love you. You are the only other person who can instruct my Reverb!'

Jim blushed, and began to unbox the smart home security package that he had recently purchased but not yet got around to installing. It wasn't long, however, before Sarah grew bored with his passion for technology and gadgets and interrupted her brother, asking him if there were any more prawn crackers and getting up to find them before he had a chance to respond. Jim took the hint and changed the subject.

It was good to see Sarah and Nova getting along so well, and for a moment it was as if so many years hadn't really passed and they were still young. The two women teased Jim about his mystery solving activities, calling him 'Sherlock Swimmer' and laughing. He shrugged this off, declaring himself to be the worst detective ever; he had found out nothing about the hit and run accidents- why would he, a part-time taxi driver had no authority to question a person's whereabouts- and he had just got a message from poor old Susan saying that Lara the cat had gone missing again! This led to more gentle teasing on Jim's part, with Nova asking whether she needed to be jealous of yet another of his exotic lady friends. This made Sarah ask about Nova's mystery admirer, who was leaving carnations on her doorstep; something that Jim had no previous knowledge of. He was annoyed that this was the first that he had heard of it but Nova merely conjectured that she was sure that it was harmless and that no cards were left with the flowers, and so they might have been intended for the Professor. Sarah interjected and claimed that this was not really a possibility, as they were left both at the family home and at the bookshop. Nova was clearly not comfortable with the topic of conversation, and Sarah, sensing that she may have inadvertently broached a topic that was inappropriate for the occasion, used her diplomatic skills to steer the conversation onto a different, less awkward, subject and the relaxed, light hearted atmosphere of the evening immediately returned. Nevertheless, the night inevitably came to an end and Jim insisted on walking Nova home and treasured the minutes they spent alone, walking briskly along the cold, deserted streets of Brockford.

The next day Jim was abruptly woken up by the words of another person, for the first time since he had been home. It was strange, he thought, how quickly he had become accustomed to the sounds that the empty house made. His Reverb did inexplicably start talking once or twice, but that didn't really count. He thought that the presence of another person would irritate him, but it didn't. Sarah knocked on the bedroom door and, once he had declared that he was decent, she entered the room holding a steaming hot mug of tea.

'Sorry to disturb you,' she said apologetically, 'but I have to be off early today and we still have a few things to sort out. Oh, and you might want to start planning a life under the sea...America has apparently elected the first orange president so it might be the safest place. They say a lot of Americans are planning to move to Canada...what a year! First Brexit, then this...Dad would have loved all this drama, surely history will look back on 2016 and pinpoint it as the year where so much changed. Not necessarily in a good way, but a pivotal moment, he would say. And Mum would just be disappointed that the first female president wasn't elected, because, you know, if a woman was in charge there would be no more wars and everyone would be friends! And she would conveniently forget how much she hated Thatcher the milk snatcher all those years ago...Sorry, bit early for both history and politics. Have some tea. Any plans for Christmas? I say it every year, but you are welcome to come and stay with us...unless you have a better offer, of course...' Jim let her talk uninterrupted, although he thought that she was wrong, that his father would have followed the news and the updates but wouldn't have enjoyed it at all. He would fear for the future; he always wanted a happy ending and despised the contrariness of some academics who seemed to be looking to make a name for themselves through controversially contending any accepted thesis. And his mother was all for women in politics because they were underrepresented, she felt, and needed their interests to be considered. She was an intelligent woman, admittedly a little conservative, and would articulate her opinions confidently and not care if anyone disagreed- very much like Sarah, Jim thought, although she would deny any similarity.

Sarah explained to Jim that she had packed up all their parent's papers into folders that she would take home with her and sort through in the evenings when the children were in bed. This made sense, as she was always the most organised of the two siblings, so Jim didn't object. He was both sorry to see her go and happy that he could now please himself. He was relieved that his sister was keen for him to update the house as he saw fit, and vowed to make a start soon. He would talk to Nova at lunchtime, he decided, if she was free. After all, he thought, someday soon she might even move in with him; if only he could find the right time and way to broach the subject. Would she really be happy to stay in Brockford for the foreseeable future? She had talked briefly about the possibility of taking over the lease on the bookshop as the current owner was due to retire, but she hadn't seemed sure that this was a viable option. Were her concerns merely financial or did she have reservations about settling down in a town where nothing much happened? It would be insensitive to ask outright now, but maybe he could test the water a little

11
THE IMMORTAL GAME

The day following Sarah's departure, it was back to work at Odin's Cars for Jim Swimmer. He had taken on a few extra driving shifts with the November weather turning cold and wet, and the remainder of his time was spent in his study, placing Maitland Green in precarious situations, researching strange ways to conceal crimes, or, if he was lucky, on intimate lunchtime assignations with Nova Anderssen.

Jim's unjustified reputation as an unofficial mystery solver had not waned at all; in fact, due to his having taken a few days leave there seemed to be a backlog of requests. As always, Jim said that anything he discovered would be handed over to the police, or, if the infraction was minor and likely to be a one off he would have a quiet word with the instigator. Quite often, an activity would simply stop but Jim Swimmer's intervention would be suspected and he would be credited with resolving a situation. His protests were interpreted as humility. One man was understandably irate, having no choice but to take taxis for the time being as his car had been stolen from outside his house, in broad day light.

'I mean, no one saw anything, and I am on the phone to the police and the insurance company, but no one is in a hurry to sort anything out. In the meantime, I am getting lifts to work when I can, but I am used to coming and going in my own time. You don't realise how dependent you are on a car until you lose it. Just sailed through its MOT as well…full tank of petrol. And the police, well, you know they reckon it will be eleven days before they get a chance to look through CCTV footage, and by then it could be anywhere. Bloody frustrating. Look, I have a picture on my phone. Lovely little motor, it might not look fancy but it has never let me down,' he said, neither pausing for breath or seeking confirmation of Jim's interest.

All Jim could do was take a note of the make and registration and assure his customer that he would keep an eye out on his travels and spread the word, just in case the vehicle should be abandoned locally.

At just before eleven o clock in the morning of November 11th Jim pulled over onto the side of the road and observed the two minutes' silence, as always. He had parked in a layby near the top of the hill, a popular viewpoint, and looked down on the town of Brockford. He thought of his father, the historian, who was born 14 years or so after the First World War ended. It didn't seem possible, it seemed so far away, especially when the Second World War was rapidly slipping out of the scope of living memory. His father was a liberal who talked about democracy, and what it meant. It was more than just a system of voting, he would say, that is just part of it. It is about human rights, equality in the eyes of the law, active participation…those who vote once every four years and then just walk away do not understand the basic tenets of democracy, he would argue. As a youngster, Jim felt like he was being lectured, but he could always understand the importance of teaching children history. Not so much ancient times, or the Tudors or that sort of thing, but of more recent history. The late twentieth century was now history; his childhood was history. What was that quote about history repeating itself? It was a sad and depressing thought. As he was preparing to drive away, he looked over his shoulder to check his blind spot and noticed a dark red car, parked badly as if it had been recklessly discarded. It couldn't be! He checked his notes, and confirmed that it was the car reported stolen. It appeared to be undamaged, and rather than contact the police station directly he decided to phone Julian, who said he would let the appropriate department know at once and then reminded Jim that they should meet up for a couple of drinks soon. Jim promised to call to arrange a time and date, and hinted to Julian that he hoped that his name would be kept out of the reports. He truly hadn't done anything, and he certainly didn't want to become known as the go to man when a vehicle went missing in future. He wasn't running a detective agency, after all. Of course, Jim's name was mentioned and his reputation as an investigator was unintentionally enhanced because of this chance discovery.

As was typical around this time of year, darkness fell early and it was a little past six thirty when he stopped in a small carpark just outside Brockford to check his phone messages. The quietness of the Prius engine when using battery power meant that he was often unseen on arrival. Stealth mode, it was often called. Sometimes this was a good thing, but not always. On a couple of occasions, he had driven along Nova's road at night, almost silently, in the hope of catching a glimpse of her 'admirer', or possibly her stalker. Who knew where the line was drawn nowadays? He had parked for a few minutes at a time, but soon moved on as he knew deep down that he was acting inappropriately and in danger of damaging his relationship if he were to be discovered. It was not a crime to leave flowers. Some people would even say it was nice gesture. Jim suspected Adam; he was always friendly and keen to speak to Nova, always laughing or having quiet words in the kitchen. But he was the type to be upfront, wasn't he? He was a good twenty years younger too, at a guess. Jim wasn't sure, but he felt something wasn't right about him. As he looked up from his phone he noticed a figure, a man he assumed, open the boot of a silver car a few lengths in front...As the man moved closer to the edge of the car park he saw that it was Susan's inquisitive neighbour, carrying a small box which he subsequently deposited in the bushes before running back to the car and driving away. Maybe, Jim thought, he should have kept his lights on as this would have deterred him from fly tipping. There had been a recent spate of rubbish being dumped after the local waste and recycling centre had introduced charges for the disposal of certain items. Another minor crime which would result in a penalty fine if only there were the resources available to investigate and prosecute the perpetrators. Jim sighed. He guessed that it was only a matter of time before someone asked him to search through a pile of rubble in search of clues. Curiosity got the better of Jim, and he was thankful for this as when he approached the box a distinctive Persian cat immediately jumped out, which he could only assume was Susan's missing pet, Lara, although the collar was missing. He couldn't leave the poor creature near a main road, but try as he might he could not entice the cat to return to the box. Jim wasn't good with animals, had never owned a pet. He called Nova, who immediately drove down with a borrowed pet carrier and some treats to tempt the terrified feline. Nova accompanied him back to Susan's house, and she went inside to speak to the distressed woman who had been frantically calling out to Lara for most of the day. With Nova as a witness, Jim was forced to take control of the situation, so he went to the neighbour's door with the empty box. There was no answer, although the silver car was parked outside the property. Jim went back to his car, took out a pen, tore out a piece of paper from the back of his notebook, wrote a note in large capital letters and put it through the letterbox:

WE KNOW WHAT YOU DID. IF IT HAPPENS AGAIN THE POLICE WILL BE INFORMED.

He left it unsigned and hoped that the warning would prevent it happening again. It is what he would have said to his face. No need to tell Susan what had happened, and what had more than likely happened before. They could only speculate about the motivation for such a malicious act, but making a poor old lady feel insecure in her own home was unforgivable. Police involvement would surely only result in a verbal warning or a slap on the wrists. Plus, it was only Jim's word and he would have to admit that visibility was poor in the car park.

He went to the summer house that night and spoke to Walter about the old days, about history and the past and what was prescribed for the future. Walter advised that the malicious neighbours name was Gerald, and that he was a keen gardener and known to dislike animals. He was often seen at the local garden centre buying any pest deterrent that he could get his hands on, with most of them proving to be ineffective. It was possible that he just didn't like the animal using his garden as a toilet, but lacked the courage to complain explicitly. Jim took this opportunity to express how he regretted leaving the note, an act which he hoped wouldn't be something that would come back to haunt him later. It might be construed as threatening or an aggressive act. Walter tried to reassure him; a confrontation would not necessarily have achieved anything, he advised, and Gerald was a divorcee living alone; he was not generally well- liked. And more importantly, Gerald was in the wrong, so why would he draw attention to what he had done by complaining about a note?

Jim had promised to keep Walter up to date with the World Chess Championship, just starting in New York. A Russian challenger was taking on the reigning Norwegian champion; a potentially great story with Magnus Carlsen arguably being the best player that has ever lived, but it was barely covered in the mainstream print media. Walter expressed his doubt that he was greater than Garry Kasparov. It was touted as the match for the smartphone generation, but 360-degree camera views with live chat and virtual reality streaming were not for traditionalists like Walter, who didn't even have an email address. In the event, there was nothing of note to report so far; two games played, two games drawn, standard gameplay, both playing it safe. Walter talked about the 1972 world championship match in Reykjavik, between the American Bobby Fischer and the Russian Boris Spassky; the drama, the tensions, the political machinations. He made it sound like one of the greatest stories ever told. Walter laughed when Jim said that he was born in 1972, forty-four years ago, and said it seemed like only yesterday. Walter went on to explain that FIDE was now corrupt, had been for many years, and described how he went to Hastings a few years ago where the local chess history was barely alluded to, just a few sculptures here and there. He talked about the Immortal Game- appropriate in a year of so much death, and how it was played in Simpsons in the Strand, in London, where, he believed, the board was kept. The victor famously sacrificed his bishop, two rooks, and finally his queen to deliver checkmate in 23 moves. A friendly, unofficial game, not intended to be recorded but which is still talked about 165 years later. What makes a game of chess immortal? Daring attacks and sacrifices, as was preferable in the romantic style of play popular at that point in the nineteenth century? Jim guessed that it provided proof that the most valuable pieces are those that are active.

Better to take a chance than play it safe, be protected, hiding in the shadows.

As they played, Jim took advantage of Walter's talkative mood and asked if he knew anything about the McDougall family, explaining that Thomas's recent erratic behaviour and mood swings had unnerved him a little. A stress-free job that he didn't need had become unpleasant and unproductive in terms of research. Jim was on the verge of resigning every day, but somehow didn't quite do it. The arrangement was informal, and he wasn't required to give notice, as far as he knew. Walter paused, contemplating for a few seconds, and then replied in his typical authoritative manner.

'Well, you know it was always the boys and the mother...she passed away quite a few years ago now, some sort of illness, and the family sort of fell apart after that. Let's go back a bit first. Jason and Thomas started the taxi company, and it seemed to be going well. But there was talk, right from the beginning, you understand. Jason was always a rogue, a bit of a chancer, but he started mixing with the wrong sort of people. He was always heading for trouble, but he never seemed to get caught doing anything wrong. There were rumours that he was laundering money via the taxi company, and that this was the reason that they fell out. Other people say he was a police informant and that this is why he died, that it wasn't an accident. You have heard about that, yes? The car was 'fixed', they would say, by the people he ratted out, or whatever they call it these days. Some will swear that he has been given a new identity and is living in a seaside town on the south coast. Me, I think he was so bored with Brockford and the petty family squabbles that he drank too much and just drove his car into a tree. Who knows the truth? Now the brother called Michael, that is a mystery. Here one day, and gone the next- a bit of a ladies' man, if I understand the term correctly, so everyone just assumed he was on to a good thing and found a himself a wealthy widow. Or maybe he renounced his ways and joined a priesthood. His mother would have liked that!'

Jim laughed to himself and thought that the latter suggestion was very unlikely. But what about Thomas? Was it simply being alone, the only McDougall left in Brockford, that made him so bitter and unpredictable? As if reading Jim's thoughts, Walter looked up from the chessboard and exhaled audibly, before continuing:

'Now Thomas, there used to be a bit of talk about him, going back a few years now, mind. They say he wasn't happy running the business with his brother; there were always lots of arguments and tension. He always had academic aspirations but never really had the chance to go to University. It wasn't that he was stupid, but he wasn't a fast learner and he had to study hard just to keep up with everyone else. To his credit, he acquired some language skills- I can't recall which ones, to be honest- and while it was clear he would never make the grade as a school teacher he did teach at an adult education centre in the evenings. He was doing well and he was always smartly dressed, happy and keen to get on with everyone. Then his mother became ill and he was still trying to balance the company books and keep both his day and night jobs going; under a lot of pressure, to be fair. Well, there was a bit of an incident. A youngish woman was taking her oral language exam with him, as quite a few were that week. He tried to put her at ease, and was friendly and chatting to her but she ultimately didn't pass with a good grade. She then made a complaint that he put her off as he was acting inappropriately and there was an investigation. He was cleared of any wrongdoing and reinstated with no marks on his record, but it changed him, you see. From then on, he wouldn't even make basic small talk, not even a good morning, with the female students… only grunt or give instructions, never smile or show any emotion. You know how aloof he can seem sometimes. As you can imagine in a town like this, his reputation became well known and complaints about his attitude ensued and he quit, supposedly to concentrate on the business but more than likely it was to avoid further scrutiny. Then his mother died and was buried in the churchyard, and a couple of years later the brother Michael left town and then his twin brother was killed in the accident. There was no funeral or remembrance service for Jason; I think that is why many people don't realise that he is dead and believe he is incarcerated somewhere. Thomas seems to prefer that explanation, and as you have noted, he can be a little bit prickly at times so it isn't something you would ask him about in general conversation. Imagine losing a twin; it must have hit him hard.'

Sometimes Jim felt that people found him unapproachable or unfriendly, so maybe he shouldn't be so hard on Thomas, who had clearly had a tough time over the years. How strange, he thought, that a person could change so much depending on environment and circumstances. Yet he knew that he bore very little resemblance to his younger self, and even the person he was a few months ago, when he was living and working in London, felt like a stranger to him. Jim manoeuvred his queen to the far-left side of the board, and watched to see Walter's reaction.

Walter looked up and faced his opponent with a look of mild astonishment. Jim's technique had improved somewhat; a fact which was proven as he had neatly managed to force a stalemate. Jim knew his endgame was weak so was very happy with this result. He confessed that he had downloaded an app which was basically a custom chess engine programmed to play like Magnus Carlsen at various ages. He acknowledged that he was currently struggling with the 'six-year-old pirate phase'. Apparently, Jim explained, even Carlsen loses to his younger self…Walter rolled his eyes but laughed and said it must be time to call it a night.

Jim lay awake that night, thinking about the past and how fortunate he really was. He had a supportive family growing up, had never had financial worries or major health concerns. He was lucky to have had opportunities to study and travel, and now he had the luxury of time. Not forgetting his relationship with Nova; it was almost too good to be true. As he finally drifted off to sleep he was jarred awake by a noise downstairs. Someone is in the house...he slowly got out of bed, the floorboards creaking as he moved. He didn't know if this was a good thing or not...it might alert someone to his presence and scare them off. It sounded like it was coming from his study...he crept down the stairs, grabbing a black umbrella which was the only potential weapon to hand. He cursed himself for not setting up the Smart Security System that he had bought online the previous week, promising himself that he would do it the next day- if he were still alive. Jim halted as the lights came on- he had installed sensors, for convenience when he got up in the night. It had only taken a matter of minutes, it was just a case of placing them and then adding them to the bridge and updating the app...he remembered that the presence of an intruder would have had the same effect on the sensors and he didn't notice anything out of the ordinary...he felt like an idiot as he flung open the study door and saw the ReverBot robot vacuum cleaner moving in a strange pattern in the corner of the room, trapped between some old files and boxes that his sister had left behind. There was a definite flaw in the design- the wedge shape was consistent with the brand but it often got, well, wedged in corners. Jim berated himself; he had forgotten that he had remotely scheduled a late-night cleaning session, but was relieved that his home was secure. Nova would find this story hilarious when he told her tomorrow, but for now he was tired and just wanted some sleep.

'Holly- cancel ReverBot!'

'Are you sure you want to end the ReverBot session??' asked the disembodied voice.

'YES!'

*

The November moon had been getting progressively brighter and peaked with the so-called 'Supermoon' making its appearance on the Monday. Jim was working from the afternoon onwards, but thought he would take a break and drive up to the viewpoint at the top of the hill and take a look- if it wasn't too busy. In the event, the sky was shrouded in a dense fog and consequently there was not much to see. This made Jim feel despondent; he added the numbers in his head; in 2034, the next time the moon would be this close, he would be sixty-two years old. Most of his life would be over and certainly the best years. If he didn't get hit by a bus, or fall ill. For the first time since he had reconnected with Nova, he felt like he was under a cloud, literally and metaphorically, and he decided that a distraction would be a good option. It wasn't fair to call Nova; things were going well but she had more than enough to deal with right now. Instead, he let the office know that it was quiet so he would be taking the rest of the evening off, and then called Julian and arranged to meet for a couple of drinks in the local pub.

This was a good call, and Jim did appreciate having a friend with so much enthusiasm for his project as well as a fair amount of inside information. Unofficially, of course. Julian was not in the best of moods, having had a busy day, but soon perked up when he saw Jim standing at the bar.

'What a day! Been rushed off my feet, some sort of flu bug going around so it's all hands to the pump. Thought I would never get away. Just spent half an hour with a woman trying to hand in lost property; if I told her once I told her a hundred times that we aren't 'Lost and Found', we can't take in items of low value or that aren't related to a crime. Haven't done for a few years now…She said it would be linked to a crime if I didn't take the bloody thing, so I was all 'are you threatening me, ma'am' and she looks me straight in the eye and says, 'Are you thick or what? Of course, I am!'. She was about ninety! I think I need a drink.'

Jim was happy to oblige and signalled to the bartender to double up his order. After making considerable progress, work on the Maitland Green stories had stalled somewhat. As they claimed a table Jim explained that he had put this project on the backburner for now as he had promised his pre-teen niece, Oli, that he would write a novella for her as a sort of Christmas gift. She wanted a novel length book and Jim felt a short story would be more appropriate so they agreed on a compromise. A novella and a gift card. Initially Jim complained, wondering why she couldn't she be materialistic and just want money like most other girls her age. Later, he realised that there was more to this request, that the most valuable commodity for this child with separated parents who both worked long hours was another person's time. Jim was aware that his sister did all she could to make time for everything and everyone, but sometimes it just wasn't enough. Cash rich, time poor. Long working hours were what Jim had escaped, and he could now see Julian's lack of career ambition in a new light.

'Help me out, Julian,' pleaded Jim, 'you have kids; what do they like these days? So far, we have a romantic period piece about a band of aristocratic vampire highwaymen in white frilly shirts and black leather boots emerging from the forest…they come across a female highwayman…a highwaywoman? But she can't be bad, she must be from a modest background and stealing from the idiot rich people for a good reason, so that she can bring out the humanity in the head highwayman vampire, who, obviously, is devastatingly handsome…might give him a scar though, to make him more interesting and likeable. I put some moralising and political content in, but then toned it right down; there is nothing wrong with a bit of trashy fantasy at her age. Pure entertainment. A chance to escape to a world where mobile phones, reality television and selfies don't exist, and we can conveniently gloss over issues like poverty and inequality. But just don't say the heroine is a werewolf or you will be wearing that drink!'

Julian laughed, and advised that this was just the sort of nonsense his daughter would read, but that he couldn't advise on the content. He then went on to suggest some hilarious feminine pen names for Jim, for no apparent reason.

'Would Jayne Swimmington like another drink? A martini for Rosanna Byron? Perhaps a snowball for Lucy Lewis?' asked Julian, tactfully disregarding some of the crude, obviously inappropriate options.

Jim advised that Oli, hopefully, was the only person who would ever set eyes on the story, which he would send to her e-reader as a document, and so no pseudonym was needed for this. However, to be serious, he did need a pen name for the Maitland Green series as he felt putting his own name on the cover would make him feel exposed. He wanted a persona to hide behind. They tried adapting names and using online name generators but every promising name they came up with seemed to sound false or was already in use. Finally, Julian asked Jim what his middle name was, and raised his eyebrows in exaggerated surprise when he replied that it was Marlowe.

'Like the detective in *The Big Sleep*?' he queried.

Jim laughed.

'Like the Elizabethan playwright! You met my parents, right?' he answered.

Julian suggested James Marlowe as a pen name, and Jim said that would do; it sounded fine. A quick online search revealed an actor with that name, but no writers popped up and so, yes that would do although he might insert an initial somewhere just to be on the safe side.

Julian returned once more from the bar, carrying two drinks carefully to avoid unnecessary spillage. He suddenly remembered that he had called in a favour from one of his colleagues who sent over copies of the report and some of the witness statements relating to the accident which resulted in the death of Jason McDougall. Of course, he couldn't give Jim direct access to this information, but was able to summarise the content if he agreed to keep it between themselves. There wasn't much to say; he was staying at a guest house in the Scottish Highlands, he was assumed to be on holiday, as he was alone. The staff at the guest house reported that he was acting a little strangely beforehand, he seemed agitated and had checked out and left the property in a hurry, despite a severe weather warning being in place. It had been raining heavily at the time of the incident, and visibility and surface water would have made driving conditions treacherous. The investigation showed that there was not an excess of alcohol or drugs in his system, so that would not have been a mitigating factor. A reconstruction demonstrated that the car had been travelling at an excessive speed and that the brakes were applied suddenly, causing the car to aquaplane, leave the road and hit a tree. The car containing Jason's body was found the next day by a local gamekeeper. Nothing suspicious; the car was checked and in good order. It was just a case of careless driving on an unfamiliar road under dangerous conditions, according to the inquest, which stated that no one could know why Jason McDougall had gone out into the rain that night but that there was nothing to suggest that he intended to crash his car deliberately.

After a few more drinks and some more of Julian's anecdotes, Jim was feeling better and walked home in a much happier mood than when he had arrived. He went straight to his study and spent many hours writing non-stop; he knew how the first Maitland Green book would end. He relished the act of fleshing out the characters in detail, and suddenly all the plans and charts on the walls and windows made sense. The morning crept up on him as he had become so engrossed in his work; the rhythmic tapping on the keyboard was the only constant sound Jim was aware of as the remains of the night melted away and were replaced by daylight and birdsong.

12
CAPITAL GAINS

Jim had decided that, whatever the outcome of his relationship or his book writing, he would stay in Brockford, modernise the family home and settle there. He was getting weary of the driving game, but there was no reason for him to keep this up for much longer anyway. Uber had finally arrived in Brockford; the council had given the go ahead and, despite fears about the impact of Brexit, an influx of human resources from various countries meant that jobs were easily filled. After living in London for so long, Jim felt uncomfortable about the lack of diversity in Brockford so maybe this would be a good thing for the community. Probably not a good thing for Odin's Cars, though, as some drivers had already indicated that they might jump ship. Regardless, there was no real reason to keep hold of the London flat. Jim would make a good profit if he were to sell this and as his tenant had recently been made redundant and vacated the property this would be the ideal time to let it go. He could use the money from the sale to renovate 23 Badger Mews and still have enough left over to live on comfortably for several years. He would need to make some arrangements, clear out the property, meet with his accountants to sign some papers and so on. So, towards the end of November he asked Nova if she would be able to accompany him on a weekend trip to London; he would drive to his now unoccupied apartment on the Friday afternoon and they could watch a show and see the main Christmas lights while they were there. The property was located on the outskirts of London, approximately a twenty-minute tube journey from the centre, so it seemed like a good idea to make the most of it while it was still in his possession. Luckily, Nova could go with him, and confirmed that she was happy to do a bit of shopping while he attended meetings and such like.

He had already broached the subject with the Professor, with whom he had grown close since his return to Brockford. They would often sit together for an hour at a time and talk about scientific evidence that Maitland Green might uncover. There were no misconceptions about how long he had left to live, and Nova had just stopped working at the book shop to spend more time with him. However, there were also no immediate dangers, he was stable and spent most of his time resting so a break from each other would do them both good. There was a strong possibility that the professor would be moved to a hospice if the pain became too difficult to manage at home, but for now his thoughts were for his daughter's future. When they were alone, he spoke to Jim about the prospect of marriage and how happy he would be to see his daughter settled before he shuffled off this mortal coil. Marriage was not something that Jim objected to, but it wasn't something he subscribed to either. Relationships should be personal, he thought, and not require external validation. On the other hand, if Nova were to suggest getting married he wouldn't hesitate to accept, as she was the only person he wanted to be with. She was always the one, and he regretted not taking a chance sooner, all those years apart when they could have been a couple...maybe, just maybe- he still had his mother's rings...Jim, surprising himself, told the professor that he would give it some thought and thanked him for his help in organising the weekend away.

Although Jim had no need to book a hotel, his flat now being vacant, he had forgotten how precarious London traffic could be and at times regretted that he had not just booked a hotel in Central London and caught the train. They had brought bedding and some essentials with them so they went straight to the property and deposited their belongings before getting changed and heading to the tube station. London was busy; there were a lot of events planned that weekend, and the weather was milder than was usual for the time of year. There was a weather warning for heavy rain for the Saturday onwards, so it made sense to see some of the sights while it was still dry.

Spending the night with Nova, watching her sleep and then waking up next to her for the first time, made Jim understand how the benefits of being tied down generally outweighed the concept of freedom. Of course, relationships were hard at times, but moments like this meant that it would be worth the effort. Before they left, he had decided that he would ask Nova to marry him, and, as he wasn't sure of her current view on marriage, if she declined then he would ask her to move in with him, to make a commitment for their future together- if not now, then when she was ready. No pressure; if she said no then he would be embarrassed, disappointed, but time was relentless and half his life had been lived already, why wait? He wasn't one for grand gestures. Whenever he tried to be flamboyant he couldn't pull it off, and a cheesy public proposal wouldn't be fair anyway.

Ring in a wine glass, getting down on one knee…too clichéd. He thought about sending a text or an email- he could even add a yes/no response button- but quickly reprimanded himself for even thinking along these lines. He googled 'How to propose', but the results were all about creating a spectacle and very much dependent on being sure that the potential fiancée would say yes. Hiring a skywriter was a bit over the top. No, it was how to raise the subject in general conversation that he needed to fathom.

In the end, he needn't have worried. On the Saturday afternoon, they had spent the day at the Tate Modern Gallery, as Nova wanted to visit the new Switch House and there was also an exhibition of Modernist photography that she was keen to see. The main gallery was overly crowded and Jim felt old amongst the throngs of younger people. There were two teenage boys taking selfies in front of Mondrian's *Composition B*, while a group of girls sat on soft benches engrossed with their mobile phones, completely oblivious to the talents of Matisse, the creator of the brightly formed collage of a snail which hung boldly in front of them. Everywhere he walked people were filtering the artworks through their tablets or mobile phones- strangely no cameras- and after the second time that Jim triggered the alarms while trying not to interfere with his fellow visitor's views he simply gave up and pretended they were not there. He found himself in front of the *Babel* installation; Cildo Meireles' sculpted work formed from a tower of analogue radios, all broadcasting at differing volumes and tuned into various channels. Just noise, the levels of sound made the output totally incomprehensible. Sensory overload, thought Jim, but I would still prefer to stay in this room, alone except for the bored looking security person who seemed to be in some sort of trance. At Nova's suggestion, Jim gladly escaped the masses and they enjoyed a drink before the photography exhibition. Nova enjoyed looking at the photographs and was still talking about the Man Ray pictures when they located the lift, which took them to the top of the pyramid-like tower, where they found the weather outside brisk but refreshing. As they stood on the tenth floor, admiring the view while trying not to peer into the elegantly furnished glass-fronted residential premises opposite, Nova mentioned that her father has been dropping very unsubtle hints about marriage.

'Well, he has a point,' Jim said, cautiously, hesitating slightly. 'I wouldn't be against the idea…what are your thoughts?'

There was a pause, and Nova explained that she thought along the same lines, but that she wouldn't want a big wedding…

'… something small and discreet, a registry office with just immediate family and a few close friends. A nice informal meal afterwards, maybe at Caligari's. And I would want my father to be there so it would have to be soon. Before Christmas. If we are going to do it we'll have to make a booking as soon as we get home or there won't be enough time to give notice. *If* we are going to do it, of course!'

'So, are we getting married then?' Jim asked, then, decisively, he answered his own question. 'Well, it seems that we are- finally!'

Jim smiled and thought that maybe the 'proposal' story would be tweaked at some point in the future. It could be rewritten to make it sound more romantic, but at that moment he wouldn't have changed a thing.

*

The rain came as promised late on the Saturday night, so, once all business was dealt with, they spent Sunday afternoon shopping. Jim remembered his mother's rings, and Nova was happy to have the engagement ring cleaned and adjusted but wanted to get a new wedding band. Jim agreed, and although he never wore jewellery, at Nova's insistence he also chose a basic, matte ring which he felt would be an acceptable compromise. Jim also produced a small, gift wrapped box. Nova opened it and inside was the key to the Swimmer house. Jim had no choice but to confess.

'If the whole proposing marriage thing didn't go well, if you thought it was too soon or too old fashioned, then I was going to offer you this. As a sign of commitment. Come and go as you like. If you need a quiet space or a break from everything. Just leave the porch light on or something so I know you are there when I get home.'

As the newly engaged couple sat in a café, Nova suddenly remembered something that she wanted to tell Jim. She had forgot, in all the excitement, and it wasn't important, just one of those coincidences that you can barely believe. While Jim was meeting with his accountant Nova had been shopping in one of the large department stores when she bumped into an old-school friend who she hadn't seen for years, and the two of them reminisced about the old days, when they lived in Brockford. Jim looked vague, struggling to recall the girl, well woman now, in question so Nova had to elaborate.

'You must remember Shelley, Jim, shoulder length curly hair. Quite tall. Used to wear round glasses, until she got contacts. Good at Maths. Anyway, she had an on-off thing with Michael McDougall - like lots of the girls did back then- but they picked up where they left off quite a few years later when she moved back to Brockford for a bit. She says he had grown up a lot, but he didn't take their relationship as seriously as she did. This was about seven or eight years ago, she thinks. Maybe more. Anyway, one day he is acting a bit weird, like there is something wrong, he doesn't seem with it, she thinks he might have been drinking. His eyes are weird, dancing about all over the place and they have bit of a row; he has just agreed to go away for a friend of a friend's stag do that weekend when they had plans. Someone had dropped out so he filled the place and she gets side-lined, yet again…And that was it. She never saw him again. He just disappears and no one is interested in helping her contact him; they all think that she has been dumped, he has met someone while he was away and doesn't have the guts to tell her to her face. Ghosting, they call it now. She went to his house and Michael's brother said he would pass a message on, but she doubts he did. She said he was a bit cagey, like he was hiding something, didn't want to let her through the door. Michael's car wasn't parked in its usual spot so he probably wasn't there. Poor Shelley, she is still fuming about the whole affair. Weird, eh? Come up to London and meet someone from Brockford…'

Nova paused, and asked Jim if he would miss living near the capital city. Jim shook his head but in truth he had mixed feelings about leaving London behind. Although he liked the cultural diversity and cosmopolitan nature of the big city- the art galleries, the theatres, the opportunities, the people- he knew that Brockford was the place that truly felt like home. If the writing didn't work out, he could easily find a job locally or maybe refocus his career; try something new. Also, he planned to take some trips with Nova when things were more settled so it wasn't like he would have a chance to get too set in his ways. There would be a delayed honeymoon to look forward to, although this would happen when the Professor was no longer with them so it would be another bittersweet memory. For a moment, he felt overwhelmed by how quickly things were changing, but then he remembered that this was the new start that he had wanted for a long time and he knew instinctively that he was doing the right thing and that this was, well, not fate exactly but it was meant to be

13
FAMILY MATTERS

After the weekend, it was back to reality for Nova, who could organise the wedding in her usual efficient manner while juggling her other duties. They went to the Register Office together to give the required notice, and luckily there was a date available the day before Christmas Eve. This was just over a month away, but Nova was adamant that there would be more than enough time to prepare. Jim then just did whatever he was asked to do and was impressed by Nova's calm and methodical planning. He booked Caligari's as requested, for the afternoon of 23 December when it would usually be closed. They would have exclusive use of the restaurant until the evening opening session. He was glad of the informal arrangements; he picked the wine and champagne and advised the restaurant that they would bring some flowers and candles for the table. No other decorations were required, with the existing Christmas lights being sufficient, and a decorated tree was also due to be installed by the entrance later that week. Sarah would be driving down with the children, and, to Jim's surprise, both his nieces were delighted that they were to be impromptu bridesmaids- a non-negotiable concession to the low-key plans. It was a shame that they couldn't stay overnight, but Jim understood that it was a busy time of year and they hadn't given much notice. Hans was coming over from Oslo and would be staying until after the New Year, and Jim was looking forward to seeing him again. Although he was just a few years younger, Jim had difficulty reconciling the quiet, fair haired boy who used to follow them around with the accomplished photographer and artist that he had been communicating with by email.

Later that day Jim stood shivering outside Odin's Cars and told Thomas that their casual arrangement was now terminated. Of course, he explained, he would help him out if he was truly stuck, if several drivers were off sick for example. He added that he would be getting married just before Christmas, and offered an invitation to come to the restaurant afterwards. Thomas didn't seem surprised and was very subdued, he mumbled something that sounded like 'very busy, work to do' and quickly disappeared into the portacabin when the telephone rang. When Thomas emerged from the office a few minutes later he was surprised to see Jim still standing here.

'Forgot to ask,' Jim said, warily. 'I was going to invite Michael to the reception. Do you have a forwarding address or a contact number for him?'

As expected, Thomas made an excuse and said that he didn't have any details to hand, and that he would have a look at home later, if he had the time, maybe. Jim didn't quite know why he asked this. Although it would be nice to catch up with him, he had no intention of inviting Michael to the wedding reception, as the numbers had been kept deliberately small.

He wondered why Thomas was always so evasive, and the next day he found out some information that might provide a possible explanation, in part. It was Tuesday, and Jim had driven to town with a grocery shopping list and the intention of buying a new suit for the wedding. A sudden downpour forced him to take cover in The Jazz Bean, where he ordered his favourite flat white coffee but courageously resisted a home- made pastry. He claimed the last vacant table, and watched through the window as the rain drenched the pedestrians caught in the deluge. 'Happy' Harry appeared in front of Jim, and asked if he might join him, observing that it was extraordinarily busy in the coffee shop. Jim acquiesced and asked him how things were going.

'Not bad, not bad. I hear you are done with the taxi game now? Surprised you stuck it out for that long, to be honest.'

Jim confirmed that he had moved on, saying that it was only ever a temporary job, and was interesting at first but had become too much of a drain on his time. They chatted informally about their colleagues and the regular customers they had picked up. Apparently, a few people had hoped to be picked up by 'that detective driver' but had been disappointed. They laughed. Harry became serious, explaining that he liked his job, but had some concerns regarding his employer. He had heard that Jim and Thomas were friends from way back and thought that there was something he should know about.

'You see, I found out that Thomas is heavily dependent on benzos. Various pills, he has a stash in his drawer at the office-not his name on the boxes, if you know what I mean. He's had a few issues over the years so had been prescribed them in the past, but he has taken to self-medicating-and it isn't doing him any good. I won't say how I found out initially, but we are going back years…Anyway, none of my business, I accept that, but I had to say something when his driving was getting erratic. I saw him jump a red light once, and another time he fell asleep at the wheel. No excuse for getting behind the wheel if you aren't in a fit state. He of all people should know better- after what happened with the church crash all those years back. Anyway, he didn't take it well, fired me on the spot but I do need this job so went back when he came around and apologised. Said he was getting help and I agreed to keep it between us, so long as no other incidents occur. I am breaking the confidence because you two go back so far and he needs someone to look out for him- and I will have to inform the authorities if he doesn't sort it out.'

Jim didn't know what to say. Maybe that would explain the blank look in Thomas's eyes, the slowness to respond at times, the evasiveness...Of course; the church incident. Jim wasn't living in Brockford at the time, but he heard about it. Michael McDougall was driving Thomas home after a night out and had crashed into the stone wall outside the church. Thomas still walked with a limp as a result of a particularly badly broken leg. Michael came out unscathed, except for a drink-driving conviction and a moderate fine, and the episode was soon forgotten.

'I will give it some thought,' he replied.

Jim wondered if Thomas could have been responsible for some of the driving complaints he had listened to. The red light, the hit and run...Although he rarely picked up passengers, he had access to the company taxis and often borrowed a vehicle when it wasn't being used. He could cross reference some dates and times, descriptions; maybe there would be something in his notebook to confirm or refute this possibility. At the back of Jim's mind was what he would do with this information if Thomas was implicated. For now, he had a suit to buy and he had promised to pick up a parcel for Professor Anderssen, which he would drop off on the way home. He would have to brave the weather, so he left Harry sitting in the warm café and went on his way.

Two hours later, Jim parallel parked in a space outside the Anderssen house, and picked up the parcel resting on the passenger seat. It wasn't heavy. He picked up a second small box, containing small pastries from the town bakery. The Professor had a small appetite these days and little treats encouraged him to eat, which pleased Nova. As Jim approached the front door he wasn't best pleased when Adam flung open the door and greeted him with a cheery smile. Although not usually a jealous person, Jim felt suspicious of the way Adam always seemed to want to get Nova on her own for secret conversations, and he wasn't the regular carer. It didn't help that he was conventionally handsome, well-groomed and, although he was no fashion expert, Jim could see that he had a keen, effortless sense of style. Adam was a volunteer, he wasn't paid to be there but he was there all too often. The Professor was a nice guy, fun and quirky and everything, but still…

'I hear congratulations are in order! You did well there, mate, punching above your weight a bit but gives hope to the rest of us, hey? Only joking, you two make a fab couple, made for each other. Kettles on; Professor Lars is waiting for you in the front room. I'm offski, running late, so you're making the tea!'

Irritated, Jim muttered a quiet thank you but went straight to the kitchen to make the tea as commanded. Professor Lars indeed! He arranged the pastries on a plate, and then entered the lounge, carrying two mugs of tea. The Professor was sitting in his favourite bright red armchair, with his feet resting on a matching footstool. He continued to wait patiently, not moving or speaking at all, while Jim returned to the kitchen to retrieve the plate he had carefully laid out. The Professor waved the plate away as Jim offered it to him.

'Maybe later, Jim. I am not very hungry right now. What do you think of Adam? He is a nice lad, good with people and very generous with his time. Bright, too, although he dropped out of University. He is a Care Worker at Forest Lodge, but I have asked Nova to talk to him about going back to his studies. He should be a nurse at least; the National Health Service needs people like him desperately. I shouldn't interfere, I know, but I keep nagging her to give him information about degree courses and funding and so on. He reminds me so much of Hans when he was younger…Not in looks, but in his mannerisms. I do miss him. I wish I were well enough to travel.'

Nova would do anything for her father right now, and Jim felt foolish, feeling that the Professor must have sensed his jealousy. Of course, it was so obvious. Nova had been a career advisor at a University a few years back so she would know exactly where to find information on courses and funding routes. If only he had asked she would have told him this, but he didn't want to come across as over-protective so had avoided the topic and created in his mind a connection that wasn't there. Surely, if anyone were to be leaving her flowers it would be Thomas McDougall, he used to have a crush on her when they were teenagers, hanging out together. He remembered; they used to laugh about it, secretly. Their code for him was 'TMD'. If they saw him heading in their direction they would usually hide until he passed. It was a running joke that he always agreed with everything Nova said or wanted to do. He always wanted to sit next to her, so they would always try to engineer things so that this was not possible. He once gave her a box of chocolates when she was ill. Nova thought nothing of it, and gave them to one of her friends as they weren't to her taste. Later, her friend was bemused to find a romantic note hidden under the lower tray. What could Nova say? They looked to be sealed. She laughed it off as someone in a chocolate factory having a joke, and never said anything about it to anyone other than Jim. How could Jim have forgotten all this? Coming to think of it, not many of the group were particularly kind to Thomas; only his twin Jason stood up for him. And Jason was, well, not someone you would want to upset.

'Penny for your thoughts,' interjected Professor Anderssen.

'Just thinking about Thomas McDougall. About when we were growing up, and something someone said earlier.'

Jim reiterated what Harry the taxi driver had said in The Jazz Bean coffee shop. The Professor was thoughtful. He recalled Nova telling him about the conversation he had with an old friend in London, about Michael McDougall before he disappeared.

'Remember, the lady he was with said he had weird eyes, they were dancing about all over the place, or words to that effect. It made me think of a condition called Nystagmus, a symptom of this is rhythmic involuntary eye movement- sometimes the term 'dancing eyes' is used. Some people have it from infancy, some acquire it later, but it is also caused by many other factors...such as toxic poisoning, brain tumour or benzodiazepine overdose. Now, she said he was not with it, and she thought he had been drinking- maybe his speech was slurred. Sounds like it could be benzodiazepine toxicity to me...They used to prescribe drugs like diazepam and temazepam a lot more freely back in the day, and from what Nova has told me Thomas has had a lot of physical and emotional problems over the years. It is not inconceivable that he would buy these drugs over the internet or from some other illicit source if a doctor cut off his supply. Or he could have just been drinking or abusing drugs himself and we need to stop thinking like Sergeant Maitland Green!'

Jim laughed, 'So, are we saying that Thomas McDougall poisoned his brother- for what reason? And where is he now- alive or dead? Did Michael ever leave the McDougall house?'

They had precisely no evidence to suggest this was the case, just a half-baked theory. The only conclusive thing they could say was that there was something not right about Thomas. Jim told the Professor, in confidence, about how Julian had gone through the reports and investigations regarding Jason McDougall's accident, and that there was no chance that it was deliberate.

'He must have died around the same time as Michael was last seen in town, but we know Jason was in Scotland and Michael was here in Brockford, as was Thomas. There can't be any link,' Jim explained.

The Professor suggested calling in one last favour; ask Julian to use police connections and resources, if this was possible, to track down Michael and then there would be no more speculation. Jim nodded and asked the Professor if there was anything he needed before he left him to rest. It was probably nothing but he would have a word with Julian when they next met.

As promised, when he arrived home Jim printed out some articles for Walter regarding the New York chess championship, and as things were a little more interesting he was keen to see his reaction. After a series of draws, the Russian challenger, the underdog, had taken the lead after the reigning champion resigned after 52 moves and 5 hours of play. Karjakin was up against the clock and risking instant loss, once nearly running out of time after making his move with just seven seconds to spare. Carlsen took this loss badly, refusing to attend the press conference after throwing up his hands and leaving the stage before his opponent arrived. Jim saw this clip online and it saddened him, made him feel a little sick; he could imagine the joy that Karjakin felt at his success, but was more familiar with the disappointment and self-criticism that Carlsen would be imposing on himself. He hoped he could turn things around, even though he previously didn't have any preference for a winner.

When he spoke to Walter that night, Jim asked Walter about his family for the first time. Walter told him that he was the last one of his family left; he had never married and had children, and had no living siblings, so Jim did not pursue the line of conversation and merely stated that he missed his parents but was grateful for the family- and friends- that he did have left.

14
POSITIONAL ADVANTAGE

Carlsen managed to capitalise on Karjakin's errors to grab a win on the tenth game, ensuring that the two players remained on a level playing field. After willing Carlsen to win, Jim felt bad for the young Russian, noting the look in his eyes as he realised the impending defeat. Two subsequent draws had meant that they would go to a tie break round of rapid chess; to Carlsen's advantage, Jim thought, but he was far from an expert commentator. Karjakin seemed to struggle with time constraints, and Jim knew what that sort of pressure could do to a person. He had promised to let Walter know once he had news and cursed his elderly friend for not using a mobile phone or having email access. Walter did, in fact, own a mobile phone but it was kept in a drawer and had never been used.

'Too complicated, too late for me to learn new things at my age,' he had said.

Jim had responded by pointing out that Thomas Pynchon has written about the deep web and internet conspiracies when he was nearing his eighties, but Walter looked blankly back at him and declared that postmodernity was not really his thing, and Jim could see that there was no point in pursuing the discussion any further in this direction. Single mindedness was a common trait in the older generation, he thought, and he wondered how long it would be before he himself became set in his ways. If he weren't already…It was fortuitous that Jim's mother had left an old-fashioned address book in a drawer, and he quickly discovered Walter's home telephone number written in ornate cursive script on the final page. Jim didn't even know Walter's surname, but was glad to be able to call and invite him over to the house to watch the final online. Walter accepted, but insisted that they stick to tradition and meet in the summerhouse.

Following the tenth game there was a day of rest for both the players and for Jim, who felt that he should use this free period carefully as he would soon have to be more generous with his time. Looking for inspiration, Jim decided to read through Julian's notebook at long last. 'Let's see what we can find in The Brockford Files', he thought to himself, and settled down in front of the fire, much as his father used to when he was reading the newspapers.

Jim forget to heed Julian's warning about opening the notebook carefully and a large pile of newspaper clippings fell out and landed in a pile by his feet. Julian's son had been quite a serious collector, if not methodical in his arrangement of the articles and photographs. They went back several years, from long before the boy was born and stopped three or four years ago. Jim sorted through the pile on the floor and put the more interesting ones to one side. Lots of ideas that he could use, adapt. He found an article about the car accident involving Thomas and Michael McDougall, but there was nothing there that said anything new. Just a grainy photograph of a car nestled amidst the wreckage of a wall, with the old church in the background. A few other articles looked like they might be interesting. He was about to discard a court report from the wider County newspaper when he saw the sensational 'love triangle' headline- *not the sort of thing Maitland Green gets involved with if he can help it*- when he stopped. The photograph of the woman on trial looked familiar; the article was over twenty years old but the face was very clear. It couldn't be? Same first name, different surname but that was Susan, the cat lady, looking nonchalantly back at him. She looked much younger in the photograph; she had clearly not aged well. It seemed that she and her sister had been interested in the same man. He ultimately decided to marry her younger sister. According to the report, Susan appeared to accept this and remained on good terms with her sister and brother in law. However, over a period of ten years she surreptitiously sustained a campaign of vengeance against those who had wronged her. It started with little things, minor inconveniences but soon escalated. She would plant phone numbers, random photographs or women's underwear in her brother in laws suit pockets when she went upstairs to use the bathroom. She would call his workplace and make anonymous, outrageous claims, causing him embarrassment and unwarranted damage to his reputation. She tried to convince her sister that she was a poor wife and an unfit mother, slowly chipping away at her self-esteem. There was basically a catalogue of malicious acts, which culminated in the poisoning of the man who had not only rejected her but taken her sister away. Susan worked in a medical laboratory and managed to acquire a small amount of ethylene glycol, the toxic chemical in anti-freeze. It was claimed that she laced a cocktail with the colourless, odourless liquid, which she then gave to her brother in law, who found it too sweet and only sampled a small amount before tipping it away. This act saved his life, although the damage done to his kidneys was severe, and would limit both the length and quality of his life. The evidence against Susan was overwhelming, but still she tried to pin the blame on her innocent sister. She received a long sentence, but that would have been served by now. And the strange thing, which made Jim feel rather edgy, was that her sister's name was Lara. Jim was glad that he had declined a cup of tea last time he visited. People change, of course, and she had served her time. Still, he was determined to avoid going there again, and now that he wasn't a taxi driver he should have no reason to. Any cat related problems would be referred to the local feline charity. And she seemed so vulnerable, so innocent.

Jim had some difficulty in deciphering Julian's handwriting; maybe he would get him to read through the notes with him some time. The Brockford File would have to wait for now, anyway. Jim had just had an idea for the second Maitland Green book; he hadn't finished the first one yet but he had to make some notes at the very least…

The last day of November arrived and that evening, as agreed, Jim sat in the summer house with Walter until gone midnight, huddled beside an oil filled radiator and watching the tie break games on his tablet. Jim created a personal hotspot using his mobile phone specifically for this purpose but stopped short of trying to explain tethering to Walter, who just had no interest in that sort of thing. Not wishing to pay the subscription required for the visual feed, they watched the live board animations on a constantly updating webpage. Walter was almost sold on the merits of technology, with the excitement of watching the clock tick down as the challenger almost run out of time. Jim or Walter would suggest the next move and then watch as the player did something completely different. However, sometimes the players made their move so quickly that black and white moved simultaneously, and they would have to double check the notation to confirm which move was made. Walter was in his element with his notebook and pen. The champion secured a victory on the third game, and so just needed a draw on the fourth and final game, and it was agreed that, barring a catastrophe, Carlsen had retained his title at that point. Walter was pleased with the outcome, and said that the correct person had won, but expressed his opinion that the Russian would challenge again at the first opportunity and that he had the aura of a future world champion. Jim pretty much agreed with his assessment, but they were both a similar age, and both had the potential to improve their technique or develop a strategy for keeping control when under extreme pressure. Only time would tell.

Jim changed the subject and recounted how his father had wanted to install a wood burning stove for the winter months but his mother had objected, fearing that it would be a fire risk. He had no idea why he recalled this now, although it might have been the fact that Walter had objected so strongly when Jim had suggested moving their games indoors, inside the main house. Walter remembered this conflict, and talked about how Sylvie Swimmer had changed after Jim's birth; she had a difficult time and there was a lot going on. She became anxious, more tied to the home and was preoccupied with preserving the family life she felt was so precious. He added, rather cryptically, that he supposed she had the positional advantage. Walter paused and it appeared that he was about to say something else, but just then Jim disrupted his flow when he involuntarily yawned, and subsequently made his excuses to leave. Since he had begun seeing Nova his insomnia had gradually improved and was now only intermittent, which meant that he now often yearned for a full eight hours sleep each night.

15
COLD AND FROSTY MORNING

The first day of December heralded a frost so severe that it could have been mistaken for snow at first glance. Jim looked out of the kitchen window and noted the white powder clinging around the edges of the window panes in the summer house, and thought that it was strange to refer to it as a summer house when the icy cold winter was evidently waiting in the wings. The day had also started strangely when Jim received a message from Gerald, the cat-napper, asking if he would be able to pop over and give him some advice. Fearing that this was a trap of some sort, following the anonymous note that had been left for him, Jim reluctantly said that he would drop by later that morning for an informal chat.

On arrival, Gerald invited Jim into the enclosed porch and asked him if he wouldn't mind removing his shoes. Jim did so, although he was wary in case he needed to make a quick escape. The interior of the house was excessively neat and cleaned to a standard that even his sister Sarah would admire. Everything was organised and symmetrical and Jim could detect the tell-tale signs of obsessive compulsive disorder. Did Walter say that he was a divorcee or did Jim hear that from someone else? Regardless, this was a child and pet free home, Jim could see that, and he believed that Gerald wasn't exactly happy to have admitted a visitor, even though he had made the request. They talked quietly, and Gerald spoke about the note that was left, conveniently omitting much of the story, and Jim was relieved to find out that he was not suspected of any involvement. In fact, Gerald had been in the shower when the note was left and so was unable to answer the door. The anonymous note, he explained, was the most recent event in a catalogue of minor, but disturbing, occurrences. Small acts of vandalism, things thrown into the garden. Mud smeared over his car. Silent phone calls. Unsolicited mailings, mostly junk and circulars but addressed to him personally. Not something that he would typically bother the police with, although he had once called the non-emergency number after a particularly stressful day. If Jim hadn't been a witness to his cat-napping actions in the car park, then he would have been more sympathetic and would have felt sorry for this anguished, lonely man. Jim asked if he could have the note, and was massively relieved when it was handed directly to him without question or suspicion. Jim would shred it as soon as he got home and say it was lost if asked. It was probably just kids, playing silly games, Jim advised. The calls might have been made by an auto dialler, nothing malicious, and so he advised of services to restrict this type of contact. Keep a diary of incidents for a couple of months, Jim continued, and maybe we can go over it and look for some patterns or clues.

Jim was sure that he knew what was happening. He had discovered Susan's criminal past through the newspaper article and this, combined with some hearsay provided by Walter, indicated that the antagonism between the two neighbours was an ongoing feud of sorts. Susan was not as frail and vulnerable as she made out, and was deliberately tormenting Gerald at every opportunity. And Gerald, well, he wasn't exactly being upfront either.

*

Gerald was playing a game. He wondered: did Susan know that he had taken her cat? Probably not; she wouldn't have believed that he would get his hands dirty! But then she left the note; she must have guessed that he removed the cat after the second time, maybe she saw something although he was careful; he had even thrown the collar into a random wheelie bin. He had to use a lot of hand sanitiser afterwards. A hell of a lot. He would never harm an animal, but God he hated that cat and the excrement it left on his lawn, the half dead birds ...and it would just look at him with no fear in his eyes as he tried to chase it away. He had tempted it with prawns laced with a mild sedative, forced it into a box...He wasn't a bad person, he could never harm a living creature. Except for slugs and snails. And mice and rats. Other vermin, maybe. Anyway, people are stupid when it comes to pets, and someone would feed that stupid cat and take it in, it would be fine. But Gerald knew what she was doing; she was running a vendetta against him and making his life impossible but no one would believe the cranky, obsessive divorcee who nobody liked. So, he brought in the man who would quickly find out about her exploits; the amateur detective would expose her as a bully and ruin her holier than thou reputation. He didn't want to invite that smug man into his home- he would have to spend ages cleaning again now- but he wanted the nosy old biddy to see her good buddy saviour Jim Swimmer pull up outside *his* house in that ridiculous silent car and go inside to discuss who-knew-what, and she was sure to be tormenting herself over what was being said.

*

Jim watched Gerald's face contort as he seemed to be silently thinking. They were as bad as each other and should just be left to get on with it, he decided. It was true that he resented his time being wasted in this way but at the same time he was relieved that the note was now in his possession and that he could now distance himself from the whole situation. He thought he had left this sort of thing behind when he left London, but some of the people living in Brockford were a bit strange. Not quite 'Twin Peaks' strange, but rather odd nonetheless. Susan had an unsavoury past; a criminal record despite the upright vulnerable image she endeavoured to maintain. She was clearly reverting to her old ways, if she had ever changed. Gerald was not a nice man either, but at least they were unlikely to meet up for cocktails. Jim quickly reclaimed his shoes from the porch and saw Susan's curtains twitching as he drove off, swearing never to set foot in this street again.

16
THE SWIMMER DEFENCE

A few nights later, Jim found Walter waiting in the summerhouse but for the first time the old wooden chess board was devoid of pieces. Walter wasn't there to play, he explained, but to wish his friend well for the future. He noted that he seemed a little distracted the last time they had met. Jim reassured him that he was fine, and Walter nodded and went on to clarify that he would not be playing tonight, or any other night, now that the wedding was imminent. Before Jim could say anything in response, Walter went into a speech about the need to work on his relationship with Nova and to never take her for granted; it was time to move on to a new phase and to leave the past behind. Walter's biggest regret, he iterated to Jim, was to let the past consume him and take precedence over the present time and his personal relationships. Besides, Walter concluded, his age was starting to catch up with him and he would be moving into a care home in the New Year, where nightly absences might provoke a missing persons search. Walter reluctantly accepted the wedding invitation that was offered to him, saying that he was a tired old man who belonged in the shadows. Jim skilfully persuaded him to attend by saying that, with his parents not being present to witness the union that they had ardently wished for, he would really like him to be there; it would mean a lot to him.

Jim stood up to leave, but then immediately sat back down again. He would miss their impromptu night time chats, although he knew that they couldn't continue. There is a time for everything.

'Everyone is playing games, no one is being honest,' Jim blurted out. 'Even me. In fact, me most of all. Being dragged into petty squabbles and vendettas but keeping what I know quiet. Leaving strange notes, making veiled threats. I was playing at being a taxi driver. Then a bogus private detective- although that wasn't my intention. And now, well I am playing at being a writer and pretending to be a responsible adult, and will be dragging Nova into the game.'

Well, it was only one note, he conceded, and he wouldn't be doing that sort of thing again. The rest was pretty much accurate. He had sat down with the Professor and had a long chat about the moral implications of knowing something but taking no actions. Jim had left Susan and Gerald to their trivial games, but what if things spiralled out of control? What if someone was harmed? The Professor had reeled off a list of household poisons which could prove fatal if ingested, even in small quantities. She wouldn't get away with it; not with her history…but that wasn't the point. He would still be culpable, to some extent. Jim accepted that he would need to refer this on to some sort of neighbourhood liaison team or something. As always, Walter had some advice to offer.

'Listen, James, you feel that you are in an impossible position, backed into a corner. Life is like chess, but there is not an option to not play. Imagine the chess board. You are white; all the black pieces are all over the place, not in immediately threatening positions but they are holding you back, stopping you from taking control of the board. You can keep moving about, gaining no ground. Or you could do the smart thing. You offer black a draw; if that is declined then you resign. Tip the white king over and walk away. Then you replace the pieces into their starting positions and you start a new game with someone else, but first you carefully plan your defence. The Jim Swimmer defence. You are white, you get to move first, you choose your moves prudently and protect your most valuable pieces, and, it might not be easy, but you take out the opponent's pieces that are holding you back, or keep them at bay. You must keep your wits about you and keep control of the game. I am rambling, talking nonsense like a mad old fool, but I will tell you something: I am still playing at being an adult! You *are* a writer, I will say that without reservation, I will also say that Nova is a sharp and intelligent woman; if she didn't want a place on your board you would know about it.'

Jim sort of caught his drift. He sometimes thought of his life as a game of chess. Nova was his queen, obviously, and he was her vulnerable king, sat on the black square, virtually paralysed, hardly able to move. The Professor and Walter were his bishops, his wise counsel. Julian was his right-hand knight and 'Holly' operated as his disembodied left side knight. Sarah and Hans, he thought of them as his rooks, not close by but waiting on the side-lines to sweep in and help him if needed. He would never say this out loud, but he often wondered how he would manage when, inevitably, he was forced to surrender a key piece.

Jim admitted to Walter that he had been thinking about the possibility of turning the summerhouse into a writing room, if he were to continue in that line of work, of course. A space to be creative, away from the distractions of the house and his intensifying dependency on technology. Walter thought that this was a good idea, and said that he should be going. Jim stood up and shook Walter's hand in a gentlemanly manner, feeling that something had changed while reminding him that the restaurant had requested his menu choice for the reception meal.

As Jim walked through the door, Walter called him back.

'James!'

Jim stopped and turned, expectantly.

'Put me down for the soup…. and the chicken. No dessert.'

17
IN PLAIN SIGHT

December had been very busy so far and it was just a couple of days until the wedding. Jim felt incredibly relaxed about the whole affair, mainly because it was so informal and all he really had to do was turn up at the Register Office on time for the brief ceremony. Julian assured Jim that he would keep him on track and not allow him to be late under any circumstances. Hans would take a few photographs, but he had promised that it would not take long and so they would soon be free to enjoy a nice meal with a few close friends and family.

Nova Anderssen had been quite calm, but was starting to be anxious. She wasn't concerned about the level of commitment she was making in terms of the wedding. No, she knew that she was doing the right thing there and had no doubt that her future lay in Brockford. However, she had just told Jim and her father that she had signed the paperwork and in January the bookshop would be hers to run. She had purchased all the fixtures and fittings, as well as the existing stock. They were both pleased and enthusiastic, but she had a niggling doubt about whether she could make it work. It was a big financial risk, taking on an independent bookshop in the current economic environment. Sensing that she could do with some space to relax and think, Jim reminded her that she had a key to his house, and was welcome to go there to take some time out. In fact, he would be meeting Julian later that afternoon and going for a long walk into Badger Wood to take some photographs for the cover of his book, which was almost completed. The house would be empty and there was wine in the fridge. She didn't take much persuading, so Jim promised to incapacitate the alarm before he went out, and also disable the overly polite Reverb voice confirmation that tended to irritate Nova.

Jim and Julian met by the garage as arranged. Julian said he was thankful that it was not raining but he was also hoping that there weren't many people out and about.

'The mud should put the dog walkers off,' said Jim as his boots sank down into the muddy pathway that led into the woods. 'And it'll be getting dark soon. I reckon we'll have time to get some good photographs, if the rain holds off. By the way, I decided on the title of the book- "Little Green Men." As in the masked soldiers in unmarked green army uniforms, not the Martians from the 1970s. Well, you know what it's about; you've read most of it. Thought I might get some atmospheric photos that might be usable for the book cover. With a bit of luck, we will get some pictures of the badgers too. My youngest niece is mad about wildlife, so she will be made up if we see the ginger badger. She was telling me the proper name for it- erythristic or something, it is a mutation that affects the colouring, quite rare. The local society said that badger activity was reported over by Badger Ridge, so if we head towards there we shouldn't get lost. The path is quite clear.'

They talked about the plot issues as they walked, slowly as the soggy ground was causing resistance. Jim captured a few images on his digital camera, explaining as he did so that he usually just used his phone but thought he should get some use from the camera that he had bought on impulse the previous year. Nova's younger brother Hans was arriving the next day, and he had offered to use his professional editing skills and software to design the book cover. Jim wanted to have something for him to work with, at least.

'Little Hans, eh!' exclaimed Julian, thinking back and trying to recall the face of the young lad who left Brockford all those years ago. 'I wasn't sure he would make it over. I am interested to see what he looks like after all these years. Sounds like he has done well for himself though…Nova says he will be up for a bit of fun on your Stag Do…'.

Jim interrupted and started to object. He didn't want a fuss, there was too much to do…he stopped as he stumbled over a small branch and realised that they had just reached Badger Ridge. He turned around to take a photograph of the branch that had almost cost him his balance and his dignity but had made his friend laugh good naturedly. As the camera flash lit up the area he realised that it wasn't a branch at all.

'Julian. Look down here. It's a bone, I think, and if my grade C Human Biology GCSE serves me right…it looks like an arm bone, you know, ermm the humerus?'

A rustling noise made them both jump as they leaned forward to examine the item more closely. Julian shouted out loud.

'Shit. Bloody badgers! Made me jump. They have been digging around here it seems. Over there- there is a mound of earth, that must be where they are making a set. Let's have a look- quietly now.'

They shone their torches into the area known locally as Badger Ridge, and Jim thought it was only right that there were now badgers here. This was the exact area they used to meet when they were young, only twenty minutes or so into the woods but usually quiet and sheltered. Pieces of a partly decomposed skeleton were scattered across a small area of ground; not a pleasant sight.

'How long do you think it has been here?' whispered Jim, although there was no other person around to overhear.

'Hard to say, ten years, maybe. Not my area of expertise. We'll have to go back, I've got no signal. No, hang on Jim, I will wait here and keep the area secure; you will have to call it in. Keep walking until you get a signal and then meet them by the road, show them where to come.'

Jim walked away, and as soon as he picked up a signal on his mobile phone he called the number that Julian gave to him, and it was confirmed that a specialist unit would be despatched straight away. The forensic investigation team would soon be here, and Jim hoped they would disprove his unspoken theory that Michael McDougall was dead and had been buried in a shallow grave in Badger's Ridge. A clue was there, he could see a chunky gold St Christopher pendant lying on the ground, just like Michael always wore. It was his good luck charm, but Jim supposed there were a lot of them around. Or there used to be. There was no definitive evidence, nothing was certain. As Jim disconnected the call an alert sounded on his phone, then another, and another…what was going on?

*

Thomas McDougall was one step ahead and had accepted that the net was closing in. Thoughts were churning around in his head, muddling his actions…He had made some stupid mistakes, took some foolish risks…he never believed he was a criminal mastermind. He wasn't a bad person. He wasn't a real criminal, anyway, people just didn't understand. He had only done what he had because it was a means to an end; he wasn't a bad person…. He had been down to Badger Ridge once word was out that there was interest in the rare badger that had made its home in the vicinity. The ground was already disturbed, but there was no way that he could move his brother's remains. Too many people about, and the access was different now, since they had built the new housing estates. No way you could get close with a vehicle. His days were numbered. Now he was just set on revenge, one final act of vengeance, and the focus of his ire was the same person that it had been all those years ago. The person who always had it easy, always got what he wanted. Who ruined any chance of his getting together with his one true love. Jim bloody Swimmer. He was taking him with him.

*

Around forty minutes after Jim and Julian had left for the woods, Thomas McDougall let himself into the house using a copy of Jim's key that he had made when he was working at Odin's Cars. He had only offered him a job to get information from him; he couldn't believe his luck when he accepted. What are the chances? And when the forgetful idiot left his house keys behind, well it was almost too easy. Thomas had got a 'spare' key cut at the local ironmongers in minutes. He knew that Jim and his buddy Julian were going off into the woods that evening, so he wasn't surprised to see both of their cars parked outside the Swimmer house. That was why he was coming here now, to lie in wait in the shadows as darkness fell. There was no guarantee that Jim would return alone, of course, but Thomas didn't care. He had bullets a plenty in the gun he was holding under his coat, and what was it they called it? Collateral damage. That was it; a policeman would just be collateral damage. Killed in the line of duty. He had a family; that would be a shame, but Thomas had to grow up without a father so it was no different to that…

The porch light was on, so Thomas could easily see what he was doing. As he walked slowly along the narrow hallway the sensors on the lights activated and Thomas started and raised the gun he was holding in his hand. He swore, then froze as he heard a woman's voice coming from the kitchen.

'You're back early, did the owls scare you again…'

Nova Anderssen stood in stunned silence as she saw Thomas McDougall, dark-eyed, dishevelled and aiming what looked like a real gun directly at her.

'Shit, what are you doing here? You are supposed to be at home looking after the Professor…Shit, shit, shit. I can't think…I should have staked the house out, I knew I should, I knew it…Give me your phone- now! Now get in there and sit down, keep quiet and you won't get hurt,' growled Thomas, indicating towards the living room with his free arm.

Nova obliged, and made a beeline for Jim's favourite armchair. Thomas sat opposite, his hand shaking as he held the gun. He knew that he would never harm her, but he couldn't risk her warning her fiancée. He had thought about how she would feel once he had done what he needed to do, she would be sad for a time maybe, but in the long term it would be a kindness. She was too good for Jim Swimmer, in all honesty she was too good for him and any other man in Brockford. He noticed the landline plugged into the wall in the corner, ran across the room, pulled the cord violently from the socket, damaging the connector irreparably, and then sat back down in the same chair and his hands continued to tremble.

'Is that gun even real?' Nova asked, hoping to call his bluff

'Of course, it is! Do you want a demonstration? Jason was running with some gangster types, I knew where he stashed his weapons and ammunition. There's more where this came from. Remember the cinema shooting? That wasn't me, but I supplied the gun. Paid a kid to shoot a random guy in the car park. The plan was for the kid to do the deed while Jim waited outside for me. The kid would then meet me in the toilets and give me the gun, which I would then plant in the glove compartment of the Prius. Frame your beloved Jim. I made sure I was seen inside; I had my alibi sorted. Just wanted to get him out the way, he should never have come back. Only the stupid idiot freaked out and didn't get away; he was caught and although the contingency plan was for him to take the rap if it all went wrong, I would pay him off and see him right, it is only a matter of time before he cracks and drops me in it. It wasn't a good plan.'

Nova was stunned. 'But why? What has Jim ever done to you?'

Thomas laughed, in an exaggerated manner.

'You wouldn't understand. You don't know what it's like to be me. I had nothing growing up, no advantages, just a mum who was depressed and drank herself to death. Jason was ok, he was my twin, he looked out for me, but he was always into something dodgy. And Michael, everyone loves Mikey! He made my life a misery, always running me down, taking the piss. I know he used to laugh at me behind my back, call me names. Just having a bit of fun, he would say, but always at my bloody expense. He crashes the car and gets off unscathed, while I can't even walk properly. He never said sorry, never admitted it was his fault. Then Jim Swimmer comes back and asks about him, over and over. He ruined everything. You don't want to hear all this.'

Nova drew on her counselling skills to try and make a connection, to put a stop to this nonsense. Thomas was obviously in a mood to talk.

'I do want to hear. Tell me. I am a good listener.' Nova then asked, hesitantly, 'Where is Michael now? I heard he has a family.'

Thomas snorted.

'I go home sometimes, and pretend that all my family is around me. Mother sitting in the corner, silently snoozing. Jason, sitting at the kitchen table, fiddling with some engine parts while Michael is standing over his son, little Dougall, trying to help him with his homework. Our Michael isn't the brightest so young Dougall tells him so, saying he wants Uncle Thomas to help him…I know it isn't real, I'm not a nutter, but I like to imagine sometimes. He had the chance you know, to be a father. Didn't want to know, did he, too selfish, didn't want to be tied down. Poor girl left town, don't know if the baby was even born. I would have been a good uncle. They are all gone now anyway, only me left.'

There was a pause.

'He knew what I had done, you know. Jason, that is. I phoned him up and told him and he said not to speak to anyone, he was coming home to sort everything. That was when he was up in Scotland, he was in a bit of trouble and was hiding out. He never came back. Bad weather, he shouldn't have been on the road. Crashed into a tree and was killed instantly. That's what the police said.'

Ok, Nova thought, I'll bite. 'What *did* you do, Thomas?' she asked softly, her voice almost cracking.

Thomas didn't mince his words.

'I killed Michael. No excuses. I planned it and I don't regret it. Drugged him to make him drowsy, persuaded him that we had to bury some evidence for Jason in the woods and then I caved his skull in with a spade and buried him where he fell. I was angry; he was planning to leave again anyway. I was having a tough time and he wasn't making it any easier. Having a go at me, saying I should cut down on the pills. Wanting his share of the house for some hair brained scheme or other. I was surprised I got away with it- he clearly wasn't as popular as he thought. No one really missed him. I used his bank cards for a while. Sold his car, eventually. People stopped asking where he was, no one mentioned him for years and then Jim Swimmer comes back to town and starts asking for a phone number or a forwarding address. He knows something is up, and then there's them damned badgers! They won't leave well alone either.'

Thomas was getting irate again, so Nova tried to calm him down, show a bit of empathy while she planned the next move. She needed to warn Jim; she couldn't let him walk into a trap.

'It's not easy,' she sighed. 'I know what it's like, growing up with one parent. I was so lonely when my Mum died, I didn't even have my little brother to talk to, he went away. Could you please get me some water? I won't move, I promise.'

Thomas agreed, saying that he could see her from the kitchen so she had better not move or try anything. She repeated her promise, so he backed out of the room, keeping the gun raised and his gaze firmly on her face.

While he turned for a matter of seconds to turn on the tap, Nova reached down the side of the armchair cushion and was relieved to find the Reverb remote control in its usual place…she pressed the centre button to send a voice command. 'Schedule ReverBot -mini session- four fifty-five pm.'

Thomas turned, aggressively.

'What did you say?'

'I said I need to be back for five pm,' she quickly replied, raising her voice to be heard clearly. 'My father needs his medication.'

Thomas apologised but said that he could not risk letting her go; there was nothing to stop her exposing his plan and preventing what must be done, and further apologised that he would have to take measures to keep her quiet shortly. He didn't want her to warn Jim and give him a chance to escape- it would be for her own safety. Nova nodded; she would need to act fast when the opportunity arose. She would not be able to escape the house but she should be able to get a message to Jim, if she was clever- and if he had a phone signal out in the dense woods. In the meantime, Thomas embarked on another of his self-pitying monologues.

'I mean, why did he come back? We were getting along just fine with him out of the way. I bought you coffee, just how you liked it. I left you flowers, just like the ones you put on your mother's coffin. I was at her funeral too, but no one notices me, they never do. I have always been there for you. Waiting. I knew you would come back to me one day. I didn't think he would come back too, though, why would he, his parents were always going on about his fancy apartment and his amazing career…but no, he has brought this on himself, he should have stayed away and let me…'

'I can hear something- there's someone in the house!' exclaimed Nova.

Thomas heard nothing and was about to rebuke Nova when he too heard a noise.

'It's coming from the study- someone must have climbed through the window!' breathed Nova.

He stopped, took Nova's hands and tied them together with a shoelace and placed them carefully on her lap. He reminded her that the windows were locked and advised her not to try anything. Nova nodded; she still had the Reverb remote control within her reach and as soon as Thomas was out of earshot she planned to get any notification she could sent to Jim's phone. She would try to get his phone to ring remotely but it wouldn't work if he was out of range. Anything that would send an alert would be good, as he would pick the messages up as soon as he was away from the trees. She just hoped he would have a signal soon.

Thomas crept across the hallway, stood by the study door and listened intently…someone was moving about, there was a knocking noise as if someone was rifling through drawers, looking for something. A burglar, maybe. He took a deep breath and opened the door, at first slowly and then hurriedly, hoping for an element of surprise, and was greeted by the sight of the ReverBot, stuck in the corner as was typical, cleaning the same piece of flooring over and over. Thomas seized the device and threw it across the across the room, smashing it against the wall and yelling in frenzied anger.

*

Jim Swimmer checked his phone, which was vibrating and making all sorts of random sounds. There was an alert- ReverBot cycle terminated unexpectedly. Nova hated his robot vacuum cleaner; she would never use it. Odd. There were several emails confirming that items had been added to his shopping list. Applets run. Jim looked at the items on each email. Please. Gum. TMD. Warming. It made no sense, but Nova did sometimes have trouble making herself understood clearly when using voice recognition technology. She had a very slight accent, but…Jim remembered the home security system that he set up. The alarm was not set but the small cameras outside the property still recorded footage on a loop. Jim could access the video, it would only take a minute. He went back to almost the start of the recording and skipped though at a fast speed. He saw himself, standing outside and talking to Julian before they left. Further along he saw Nova arrive and enter through the front door; he smiled as he saw the porch light come on, but the smile completely disappeared as he saw Thomas McDougall surreptitiously approach the house with something that looked like it might be a gun poorly concealed underneath his jacket. The intruder appeared to take a key from his pocket and let himself in…Jim almost dropped the phone. It was a warning, TMD was code for Thomas McDougall, he had a gun- he immediately called the police again, running as he did so towards the entrance of the woods; he was at least five minutes away from the house and the thick muddy ground was slowing him down.

An armed response unit had been mobilised and was waiting outside the house when Jim eventually arrived. They stopped him from entering the property and told him that they had the situation under control. He showed them the footage that he had recorded and described the layout of the house and detailed the various points of entry. Before he knew what had happened, he overhead a message confirming that the police had completed their operation successfully and without casualty. It was over.

*

Realising that he would never exact his revenge, Thomas McDougall held the gun to his own head, his hands shaking, sweat pouring from his forehead and moistening his receding hairline.

'No!' Nova shouted. 'Don't.'

Thomas stood for a minute, feeling that he resembled a pantomime villain rather than a superhero's nemesis- which would have been preferable. Michael was right- he was a joke. He knew that he did not have the courage to pull the trigger on himself- he wasn't even sure that he had the ability to shoot another person. As the armed police entered the room and surrounded him he put the weapon down as instructed and allowed himself to be restrained, offering no resistance; it was almost a relief.

Thomas McDougall was led out to the waiting police car, past Jim Swimmer who was standing with some uniformed police officers, demanding to be allowed inside to check on his fiancée. Grimacing through a mass of tears, the only words that Thomas could muster were 'It's not fair…'

Jim walked past him, eager to see Nova, and simply replied, in a dull monotonous voice.

'Life's not fair.'

18
LITTLE CHRISTMAS EVE

As he was mostly on his own in the house, Jim had not been planning on decorating the house for Christmas. A few cards placed on the mantelpiece were his only concession. However, now that Hans was staying with the Professor and liaising with his carers Nova was planning on sleeping at the Swimmer house on their wedding night and insisted that it be made more festive. She reminded him that this would be their first Christmas as a married couple, and, although this year would obviously be a low-key affair, she would like some good memories to look back on. Jim agreed, and was relieved that she insisted that they wait until 23rd December, as was her family tradition, to bring in the tree and make a start on preparation for the festivities. Less time for the needles to fall. In Norway, she explained, they call this 'Little Christmas Eve'; although she believed that very few people still observed this custom. As a child, Jim recalled, Sarah would always get over excited and want to start as soon as the advent countdown began. She still decorated her house on the first weekend in December, and went completely overboard. A few minutes after agreeing to this, Jim realised that 23rd December was not only 'Little Christmas Eve' but also their wedding day! And so, it was agreed that it would be fine, under the circumstances, to prepare the house on 22nd December- and it would be a good distraction from pre-wedding nerves. It would also be a good distraction from the strange incident with Thomas McDougall and the shock of finding a body buried so close to home- especially when the victim was someone that was they all knew. Jim remembered all the noises he had heard outside at night, the times when the car alarm had gone off in the early hours, the feeling he sometimes had that he was being watched…He had attributed all of this to his imagination, lack of sleep or even nocturnal animals roaming the streets, but it was just as likely to have been to have been Thomas, hovering about, watching and plotting his downfall. Jim shuddered, and ensured that the home security system was operating correctly before driving into town.

There had recently been far too much drama in Jim's life, so as he stood in the department store feeling overwhelmed by the choice of decorations he was relieved that this was all he had to worry about for now. Julian had recommended the tacky pop-up Christmas shop- for kitsch value, of course- and Sarah had recommended sorting through the attic for gems from their childhood, but Jim just wanted something straightforward and normal, so bought most of the decorations matching a display tree and found a selection of lights. He could have done this online, he thought, but Christmas deliveries were a nightmare. He wasn't even able to get an online grocery delivery, so for convenience he went to the supermarket on the way home.

He wouldn't be seeing Nova on the eve of their wedding; she understandably wanted to spend the evening with her father, just the two of them, and so Hans and Julian were coming over to help him decorate the house and have a few drinks. Not exactly a 'stag do', but extravagant trips abroad with friends were hardly Jim's style anyway. Julian was the first to arrive, sporting an overly garish Christmas jumper that looked like it had been rescued from the eighties and a pair of reindeer ears.

'Getting into the spirit of things!' he said, smiling.

There was a pause before he continued, cautiously.

'At least 'Pyscho Tom' is locked up, well away from us all, eh? How is Nova now? Must've been a bit of a shock for her...Who would have thought? I keep thinking back and trying see how we missed it...Can't believe you left me there, freezing to death in the woods, guarding Michael McDougall's decomposing body with only the badgers for company, for God knows how long, while you were hanging out with the armed response guys! Only joking. It is him though- Michael-been confirmed. Anyway, all over and done with now, won't mention him again tonight. We won't mention 'he who must not be named' until after the wedding, as agreed. When is Little Hans getting here?'

Before Jim could answer, Hans had arrived and was standing in the doorway, somehow managing to look sophisticated in a Christmas jumper adorned with a gingerbread man as he pulled on the customary red Santa hat. He handed Jim a brown paper carrier bag, and reassured him.

'Don't worry, we know you don't like dressing up so we got you a little grey number with a discreet fair isle pattern across the top, it hardly looks festive at all...'

Relieved, Jim pulled out a bright blue jumper adorned with a Christmas tree with actual lights and, if you pressed the flashing star, 'Jingle Bells' would play in that awful tinny tone that is usually associated with socks and ties. Jim played along, carefully positioning his plastic elf ears before Hans took a photograph with his mobile phone, and a few seconds later a notification tone signalled the arrival of a photograph of Nova, looking angelic in a white fluffy jumper with snowflakes and the Professor looking pale but quirky in a bespoke waistcoat and bow tie ensemble adorned with robins, his favourite bird. They were holding up a glass of schnapps, and Hans took this as sign that a drink was needed before they got started.

'Hey, Jules et Jim- put the phone down and point me in the direction of a bottle opener- or do you have a gadget that does that for you?' laughed Hans, making a beeline for the kitchen.

And so, the evening passed, with the not-so-little Hans organising his associates and ensuring the house was suitably festive. Julian left at just past midnight, and Hans spent the night in one of the spare rooms, which had been prepared for him.

The next day arrived; Jim and Hans got ready and had been waiting inside the register office for a good twenty minutes before Nova arrived, looking stunning in an understated ivory dress encrusted with shimmering beads which suited her complexion perfectly. And the ceremony itself was brief but emotional and not once did Jim have any nagging doubts or concerns. The wedding party was small, but Jim preferred this and once safely settled in the restaurant for the informal reception he could talk with everyone and follow several conversations at once. Although he found himself briefly lamenting the missing family members who would have loved to have witnessed the marriage, he had learned that it was best to appreciate the people that were there; bitterness achieved nothing positive. Hans sat with the professor and talked about his work and his imminent return to Oslo, while Julian's children had quickly made friends with his two nieces and were looking at each other's mobile phones and laughing profusely. Probably a fat cat falling off a mountain or something inane, but it kept them amused. It was strange to see Julian accompanied by his wife and family; he seemed to be a different person, more subdued and slightly distracted. Sarah was doing the rounds and speaking to everyone in turn, and, Jim noted, spent a long time deep in conversation with Rosie. Walter got on well with everyone and kept them amused with his stories about the old days, but Jim was surprised by how slowly and awkwardly he moved. He seemed so much older, somehow. Despite the agreement for no speeches, Julian, not used to drinking so much wine during the day, stood up and said a few words and proposed a toast, which went down surprisingly well. As the restaurant opened to the public that evening, Sarah announced that she had to make a move as she had guests arriving on Christmas Eve and the children were due to spend some time with their father. Julian was the worse for wear, and so left with his family to sleep it off, while Hans said it was best that he took the Professor home. He had coped remarkably well all day, but was starting to look very tired. By eight o clock, Jim and Nova were sitting at the kitchen table in the Swimmer house, drinking tea and planning their future together. They were both glad to be staying in Brockford. Nova was determined to ensure the bookshop became a viable business prospect as well as a much-needed community facility. With Nova's guidance, Jim was planning to completely remodel his parents' house and make it their own, and had an action plan to build a new career as a writer.

For a moment, Jim felt like he was the starring character in one of those cheesy, sentimental Christmas films they show on television each year. Then he recalled the revelations and events of the last few days, which everyone had agreed not to mention for the time being. Why let it mar the wedding? He just hoped that he and his new wife would now live happily ever after.

19
SECRET PAST

Jim woke up later than usual the next day; it was a dark morning and he lay there for several minutes going over the plans they had made the previous day and thinking about when to implement the changes they had discussed. He then realised that it was Christmas Eve and decided that it was not the time to obsess over the details and that he would just drift along until the new year. Nova was already up and about, and Jim was surprised that he did not wake when she did.

He went downstairs to the kitchen where Nova was making coffee and before they had sat down there was a knock at the front door. Jim answered it and was surprised to find an apologetic Julian standing in front of him, asking if he could just have a very quick word, it was official business, he explained, but, seeing Jim's expression change, quickly added that it was nothing to worry about.

Julian explained that he would just cut to the chase; he wanted to let Jim know before anyone else said anything, but they had been trawling through some CCTV footage and building a case against Thomas McDougall. They found a lot of footage of Thomas McDougall, but were surprised to identify a second person hanging about. It had transpired that Jim had a half-brother who was just a few months younger than himself, who had been watching both him and Nova. Apparently, he was intending to make contact. Julian nervously clarified that Jim was unaware of this person's existence. Jim was shocked; he could not believe what he was hearing, his parents were happily married and there was no way this could be true. His father was his role model, always had been. It was Nova who commented that it was conceivable; she was unaware of any half siblings but she knew from her parents that Jim's parents had had marital troubles, as they called it, shortly before Jim was born. They had decided against separation and the 'other woman' had moved away never to be heard of, but their relationship was never quite the same. Jim realised that it made sense, looking back, and that there were signs of mistrust and snide comments that he had chosen to ignore. His mother had suffered from depression when he was small; Sarah had remembered this better than him. He just assumed that it was standard post-natal depression, which carried more of stigma back then and was rarely talked about. His father's lack of ambition, his withdrawal from many of his social circles, his devotion to his wife…Jim wondered if this were possibly due to feelings of guilt and remorse. Julian proposed to Jim that it was a good thing that his parents could work through their problems; his own parents had recently separated after more than forty years of marriage, much to the initial shock of the family.

'Silver splitters, they call them nowadays. It is more common than you would think. They both seem happier now. Anyway, I have had a word with David- that's his name- and he will be keeping away for now. There was nothing malicious or sinister about him, but he didn't know if you were aware of his existence so didn't quite know what to do. I have his contact details on file so I will leave it up to you if you want to get in touch with him.'

Jim's first impulse was to search through his parent's papers and documents to see if there were any clues there, but Sarah still had all the files at her house. How would he tell Sarah about this? She would find it scandalous. So many questions! Did John Swimmer know he had another son? Did his mother know? Who did he- David- look like? Jim stopped short of asking Julian for a description. He couldn't really ask the Professor; they had agreed not to mention the recent events in his presence for fear of causing him unnecessary distress. Anyway, his memory was not what it once was. Walter might know something. He was his father's close friend and confidante for many years. It would have to wait until after Christmas though, and Jim would have to locate the care home where he now resided.

'Sorry to land that bombshell on you. I will be off now- last minute dash to the shops!' said Julian, patting Jim on the back. 'Have a good Christmas.'

Jim saw him out, and was subdued for the rest of the morning. Around lunchtime, he perked up and decided that the past was not important. He turned the ring round on his finger- he still didn't like wearing jewellery but he would get used to it. He had a future to prepare for, it was Christmas Eve and he was spending it with his new wife.

Jim picked up the Reverb remote.

'Holly- play Christmas songs.'

Christmas Day was spent at Professor Anderssen's house, as he really wasn't well enough to travel the short distance to Badger Mews. Adam popped in during the afternoon to wish them all a happy Christmas and he insisted on seeing some of the wedding photographs. It was the first time in many years that the Anderssen siblings had been together at Christmas, so they made the most of it, eating and drinking, playing games and watching the usual television specials. Jim and Nova went for a walk together in the evening and she asked him if he had found the day a little boring; it was rather uneventful. Jim laughed.

'Not at all. Nice and quiet. Just how it should be.'

20
THE END OF AN ERA

A few days after Christmas, the Professor passed away during the night. His condition had worsened, so Nova had been staying with him and when Jim's mobile phone rang at around two o clock that morning he immediately knew what had happened and went straight over to be with his wife. Once the formalities were dealt with and the Professor's body had been taken away by the undertakers, there was initially silence, with no one knowing what to say or do. Jim, Nova and Hans sat up all night and talked, sometimes dozing in a half sleep, about everything and nothing. The Professor had arranged his own funeral, so there was nothing to do but notify the appropriate people and deal with the practical matters. Hans advised that he would be heading back to Oslo early in the New Year, as soon as the funeral was over. It had been a mild December in England, rather grey but nowhere near frosty enough to satisfy his Nordic tastes. Although the weather was also unseasonably mild in Norway, he still longed for the vast, bleak landscapes, the long dark days and the cosmopolitan city life. In line with the general mood, a freezing fog descended over the area, disrupting travel and causing driving conditions to be precarious for several days. Several accidents were reported and Jim was more relieved than ever that he was not required to drive people around in these conditions.

The fog started to clear in time for New Year's Eve. Jim had not planned on celebrating the event, but when Julian arrived with several spare tickets for a private function at The Highwayman Inn it was agreed that spending the evening there would be preferable to sitting indoors with limited distractions. It would also be good for Hans to catch up with everyone properly before he left, and so at around seven o clock they walked along Brockford's damp streets, amid the fading inefficient lighting which, Hans noted, was rather ineffective. Jim realised that Nova would miss Hans once he left, and so, although she would be busy with the book shop for the foreseeable future, Jim reconfirmed their plans to visit Norway in the summer. Maybe in June, to coincide with both the Midsummer festivities and his own 45th birthday. They would make time, no matter what. Arriving at the pub, they greeted the black clad security staff at the door and showed their tickets. For a brief second, Jim felt that he was back in London but as soon as they passed the threshold that feeling vanished. Jim met Julian at the bar while the others found a roomy table near the open fire- a perk of arriving early. As the building filled, various people offered their condolences and momentarily shared memories of both the Professor and John and Sylvie Swimmer, all of whom had been involved in the local community in some capacity or other. Conversation inevitably drifted onto other subjects; the spate of celebrity deaths in 2016 and the horrific acts of terrorism throughout the year were the main topics. However, the overall atmosphere was one of celebration and the distraction helped somewhat. Jim spent some time talking to Robert Jones, a local builder who had some time free in early January and could easily complete the renovations that were planned for the Swimmer house, where he and Nova would settle as a couple. Robert looked familiar somehow, but it wasn't until later that Julian explained that he was a minor celebrity in Brockford, having been on a television show a few years back.

'You must have seen 'Bricking It'? Rob the Builder was the main guy, every week they would have a DIY or renovation project that just had to be completed within a set time scale, and everything would go wrong but, against the odds, they always managed to compete the job in time. There was this inept guy who would always stick a nail through a pipe or screw the electrics…what was his name- Mad Matt? That was him. You can watch the whole series online…That was how Caligari's managed to get kitted out; there is a picture on the wall there!'

Jim did recall this now, he had seen the picture on the wall and he remembered his parents talking about the television programme. Not their usual taste, but the local connection made all the difference.

At around ten thirty, Jim stepped outside into the cold night to return a missed call from his sister Sarah, who was hosting an event of sorts with several guests. She just wanted to wish him a happy new year, she said, as it would be impossible to get through at midnight, and to check that everything was going alright. She wouldn't be able to get down for the funeral as she was unable to get the time off work, and she felt bad about this but it couldn't be helped. As he listened to her speaking he thought he saw a shadowy figure loitering under the streetlight at the end of the carpark, and he immediately thought of David, their secret half-brother. Jim hadn't spoken to Sarah about him yet; he felt guilty about keeping it from her but it didn't seem like the sort of thing to discuss over the phone. He didn't know how much she knew about the past. Jim was glad to get back inside, and Nova moved along and offered him the seat next to the roaring fire, which he gratefully accepted. He made a mental note to speak to the builder about swapping the open fire in Badger Mews for a more modern wood burning stove. Shortly after the clock struck midnight- there was an extra second in the countdown this year, but no one except Jim seemed to notice this- large groups started to leave and make their way outside, some moving on, others going home. While Hans decided to go on to a house party, Jim and Nova were glad to go home to bed.

On New Year's Day, the rain came down heavily so the fire was lit and the newlyweds spent a lazy day indoors. Jim spent a couple of hours in his study, packing up all the notebooks, documents and printouts that were not required for the time being, now that he had pretty much finished writing his first novel. Hans had created a professional cover design in less than an hour and Jim was extremely grateful for his assistance. He sat in his chair and listened to the rain falling against the window, enjoying the peaceful solitude while knowing that someone was nearby if he wanted company.

*

And so, the funeral went ahead as organised by the Professor. There was a good turnout, with friends, family and former colleagues making an appearance. The wet weather had turned bitter cold and icy, and Jim joked to Hans that he might want to stay here a bit longer, now that snow was a possibility. But Hans was ready to go home; he explained to Jim that, unlike Nova, he had never felt that Brockford was his home. Later in the day, as he drove Hans to the airport, Jim thanked him for his help and promised to look after his big sister. He said that they would look forward to seeing him in Norway the following summer- if not sooner.

The rain returned the next day, and with it the milder temperature. Jim stood at the window of his study, watching the rain batter the trees at the boundary of the garden, as the birds descended looking for worms in the newly softened grass. He had a strong sense of déjà vu, but before he could dwell on this uncanny feeling he was startled by a knock on the window. Rob the Builder and a couple of his assistants had arrived to begin the refurbishments that he had planned and for some reason had come via the side entrance, probably looking for someone to store their tools and equipment. Julian arrived shortly afterwards, regretting slightly his offer of help made impulsively on New Year's Eve after drinking more than he was accustomed to. Jim immediately put the kettle on the stove to boil; Robert's reputation as an honest and reliable builder was surpassed only by his legendary capacity for tea drinking.

'The end of an era,' thought Jim, as he explained to Julian that his so-called sleuthing days were well and truly over. Not that he was sad about this, of course.

'In future, I think I will leave everything to the police. Not that I did much anyway. I will just tell people that crimes, however minor, need to be investigated properly; by the book.'

Julian protested.

'But that won't happen, non-serious crimes will just fall by the wayside. That makes them fair game, as far as I'm concerned.'

'But I'm not playing the 'fare game' any more. I am not a taxi driver; I have no reason to be hanging around in the dark talking to all and sundry. And I have lost one of my bishops.'

Julian was confused by Jim's words but before he could ask the kettle began its high-pitched shriek, prompting a new discussion about the merits of electric kettles and smart plugs.

Jim had a lot to think about. Nova had the bookshop to run, and he had promised to help her to develop a web presence, as well as taking on the role of general dogsbody. He was also more determined than ever to continue writing; *Little Green Men*, the first Maitland Green novel was ready to be uploaded for sale, the second book was progressing extremely well and several others were in the planning stage. More had happened in the last couple of months than he could have ever imagined.

And so, as Jim watched Robert and his small crew of builders knock down the kitchen wall of his family home on a cold morning early in January he felt an enormous sense of relief; he looked forward to a quiet, ordered life in 2017.

ABOUT THE AUTHOR

Tracey Ann Clements lives in Southern England, where she likes nothing better than to spend time in her study, surrounded by her mountainous collection of books.

Four additional titles in the Jim Swimmer series of short novels are set to appear in 2017/18.

She is also currently working on a ten chapter study of the role of chess in literature and modern culture, which should be ready for release in 2018.
For more information please visit the following website.

www.traceyannclements.com

Printed in Great Britain
by Amazon

17277018R00066